D0862889

Other titles by Frank B. Linderman
available in Bison Books Editions

Indian Why Stories: Sparks from War Eagle's Lodge-Fire

Plenty-coups: Chief of the Crows

Pretty-shield: Medicine Woman of the Crows

INDIAN *OLD*-MAN STORIES

MORE SPARKS FROM WAR EAGLE'S LODGE-FIRE

FRANK B. LINDERMAN

[CO SKEE SEE CO COT]

Illustrated by Charles M. Russell

[CAH NE TA WAH SEE NA E KET]
The Cowboy Artist

*Introduction to the Bison Books Edition
by Sidner Larson*

THE AUTHORIZED EDITION

University of Nebraska Press
Lincoln and London

Introduction to the Bison Books Edition © 1996 by the
University of Nebraska Press
All rights reserved
Manufactured in the United States of America

First Bison Books printing: 1996
Most recent printing indicated by the last digit below:
10   9   8   7   6   5   4   3   2   1

Library of Congress Cataloging-in-Publication Data
Linderman, Frank Bird, 1869–1938.
Indian old-man stories: more sparks from War Eagle's lodge-
fire / Frank B. Linderman; illustrated by Charles M. Russell;
introduction to the Bison Books edition by Sidner Larson.—
The Authorized ed.
p.   cm.
Originally published: New York: Charles Scribner's Sons, 1920.
ISBN 0-8032-7960-4 (cl: alk. paper)
1. Indians of North America—Folklore.   2. Ojibwa Indians—
Folklore.   3. Cree Indians—Folklore.   4. Tales—North
America.   I. Title.
E98.F6L69   1996
398.21'08997—dc20
95-50129   CIP

Reprinted from the original 1920 edition by Charles Scribner's
Sons, New York.

LITTLE BEAR

(CHIEF OF THE CREES)

Seamed and old, the pawn of progress
  In the wicked hand of fate,
Silent, sullen, unrelenting
  In his deep, undying hate:
Hate that want brings to the haughty;
  Hate that pride alone can feel;
Hate that comes of wrongs inflicted;
  Hate and sorrow, deep and real.

Step by step and ever backward
  O'er the ground his fathers trod;
Fighting e'er, and e'er invoking
  Strength and peace from Pagan god—
Gone his greatness and his freedom;
  Grinning want alone remains;
Bison skulls and wallows mock him
  On his old, ancestral plains.

Introduction to the Bison Books Edition

Sidner Larson

The years 1880 to 1930 roughly encompass the period from American Indians losing their battle for the West until the deaths of the last men and women who had known a precontact West. During that time, a few individuals, including Frank B. Linderman, James Willard Schultz, Charles M. Russell, Frederic Remington, Walter McClintock, and George Bird Grinnell, were able to gather direct evidence and testimony from Indians who still had personal knowledge of the old ways.

Frank Linderman traveled from his childhood home in Ohio to Missoula, Montana, in 1885, a journey that enabled him to see the Old West. Although some visitors from the East, such as Remington and Grinnell, remained in the West for only a short time, Linderman, Russell, and Schultz stayed on to become important observers of the Indian country "before it was gone."

With his ability to incorporate details into his writing, Frank Linderman helped provide an invaluable service in preserving the American Indian past. While he, his good friend Charlie Russell, and James Schultz were steeped in European traditions, they were also excellent observers who respected the Indian perception of the world. Russell's painting of Blackfoot hunters returning home may be the most accurate picture we have of a Blackfoot camp in the days of the buffalo. Schultz's reflections of traditional life, gained through his Blackfoot wife and the trader Joe Kipp, have long been appreciated. Linderman's observations of Indian cultures are remarkable not only for his access, but for the way he was able to remain in the background while writing about them.

Linderman was a boy of sixteen when he arrived in the Flathead Valley of Montana Territory on 20 March 1885. For seven years he trapped in the wilderness near Flathead Lake. He married, then became an assayer, then newspaperman, then state legislator. In 1905 he moved to Helena and was assistant secretary of state. Upon leaving government service, Linderman was for a time a successful insurance salesman. Then, in 1917, in a conscious rejection of business and politics, he moved to Goose Bay on Flathead Lake to write.

Linderman's published works include four books of Indian legends, from Chippewa, Cree, Blackfoot, Kootenai, Crow, and Gros Ventre oral traditions; two novels about a free-trapper on the Missouri River, containing much information about the Plains Indians' way of life and spiritual beliefs; and two classic Native American autobiographies about the lives of Crow chief Plenty-coups and Crow medicine woman Pretty-shield.

This Bison Books reprint of *Indian Old-man Stories*, and the one of *Indian Why Stories*, lengthens the list of Linderman's works still in print. Four previously unpublished manuscripts have been published since the 1960s, including Linderman's personal memoirs, his recollections of his friendship with Charles Russell, and a biographical novel about a prairie Gros Ventre named Frozen Water, whom he called "Wolf."

Originally published in 1920, *Indian* Old-*man Stories: More Sparks from War Eagle's Lodge-Fire* is, like *Indian Why*

Stories (1915), filled with Chippewa and Cree legends. It also is illustrated by Charles M. Russell. In this book, Linderman's collaboration with Indian storytellers continues to be enhanced by his understanding of their sign-language.

Translating stories from Indian languages to English was a significant part of Linderman's work. At the beginning of *Indian Why Stories* he wrote, "I propose to tell what I know of these legends, keeping as near as possible to the Indian's style of storytelling." Linderman's method of communicating Indian storytelling was unusual for his time; it included related dialogues that took place with others besides the primary storyteller, and description of nonverbal information such as facial expression, body language, pauses, interruptions, and changes in rhythm, tone, and volume of voice.

In addition, Linderman was an early advocate of religious freedom for the American Indian, as revealed in *Montana Adventure* (1968). In 1916 he met with Chief Big Rock, a Chippewa medicine man, to gather information for his writing of *Indian Old-man Stories*. During this meeting Linderman took part in a religious ceremony that is described in the foreword. Linderman's detailed description of the ceremony, which he called a "medicine smoke," is evidence of the growing sophistication of his knowledge of Indian culture. In this, it differs considerably from the foreword to his first book, *Indian Why Stories*, which speaks much more generally of religion and customs.

Beyond the foreword, the legends in *Indian Old-man Stories* are noticeably more intricate than those in *Indian Why Stories*. There is still much surface humor in a brief story such as "Why Children Lose Their Teeth," where crabby Crane scolds *Old*-man: "I—there! You made me lose a big fish with your talking. Why do you talk so much?" Another story, "Quo-Too-Quat, the Cripple," however, runs to twenty-three pages and interweaves significant elements of Earth-Diver creation myth with its surface story of a crippled, yet very powerful hunter who saves two wayward girls.

As related in Andrew Wiget's *Native American Literature*, the past for American Indians begins in the Origin Period. In some cultures the most remotely conceptualized being is an Asexual Spiritual Being like the Aztec Ometeotl, whose dynamic self-reflection creates through thought emanation either two Sky Parents Proper (Sun Father, Moon Mother) or Displaced (Sky Father, Earth Mother). Their intercourse creates two worlds (Mountain, Water; East, West; Zenith, Nadir) requiring reconciliation. This movement of mediation can be envisioned either as an Ascent (Emergence) or a Descent (Earth-Diver). At the point of Emergence or Contact there appears a mediational figure like the Seneca Woman Who Fell from the Sky, the Navajo Changing Woman, or the Maidu Earth Initiate, whose incarnation begins the birthing of spiritual power into the present, earth-surface world, and whose body upon decease sometimes becomes the first plants and animals.

In "Quo-Too-Quat," War Eagle tells of two sisters who pretend two stars are their husbands. The stars overhear them and transport them to heaven, where an Old Woman warns them they must not stay:

> "Some stars have brought you here, but you must not stay. They are all sleeping now, but will soon awake. Come with me. I will help you. I know who you are. I am related to your mother. Those stars must not find you here. Come."

Old Woman is clearly the mediational figure mentioned by

Wiget in his discussion of oral tradition in *Native American Literature*. Old Woman saves the two sisters by lowering them back to earth on a rope of twisted bark, which is a form of descent mediation found in Earth-Diver creation myths. The addition of more complicated Sky elements to *Indian* Old-*man Stories* adds considerably to the predominant Earth elements of Trickster, birds, and animals found in *Indian Why Stories*.

Old-man is a very powerful figure, yet markedly different from Manitou, the supreme being of many Indian cultures. The figure of *Old*-man—also known as Napi and Iktomi— serves to balance the serious nature of Manitou, and represents man in his human state, restrained and often made ridiculous by his limitations, his faults, his bodily functions, and his animal nature. At the same time, *Old*-man depicts man more realistically than tragically, and draws laughter from the spectacle of human weakness or failure. Hence his tendency to juxtapose appearance and reality, to deflate pretense, and to mock excess. The judgments made by *Old*-man are almost always critical.

As in *Indian Why Stories*, an added bonus is to be found in the illustrations of *Indian* Old-*man Stories*, by Charles M. Russell. Russell's artwork, depicting Crane as well as Win-to-coo, the Man-Eater, reflects the playful wisdom that characterizes *Indian* Old-*man Stories* as well as details of a time and place that have nearly vanished from the face of the earth. This Bison Books reprint, besides being great fun to read, will help insure that the old, old West and its people will not completely vanish.

FOREWORD

IN the Preface to "Indian Why Stories" I endeavored to tell of *Old*-man (or Napa, or Nahpee, or Napi), an under-god of the Indian tribes of the Northwestern plains, especially of the Crees and Chippewas, with whom I am best acquainted.

It is a mistake to declare that the sun is the god of the Indian, or that *Old*-man and the sun are one and the same character. Nothing can be farther from the truth. The god is Manitou, and He is All — Everything — Nature; while the sun is reverenced by all tribes that I know only as the greatest manifestation of the deity, whose name is seldom mentioned.

Old-man, or Napa, created the world and its inhabitants. His mistakes and weaknesses are freely discussed, and the laugh accompanies tales of his doings; but mention Manitou and

FOREWORD

silence falls upon the merrymakers. Reverential awe replaces gaiety, and you will feel that you are guilty of intended sacrilege.

Many years ago I was in the lodge of Full-of-dew, who is War Eagle in this book and in "Indian Why Stories." He was telling tales of *Old*-man, and while all the company laughed, I remained silent. "Why does not my brother laugh with us?" asked the old warrior. I had feared to laugh at the stories lest the Indian believe that I was not serious in my desire to learn of this strange, mythical character, and I told him that. "We always laugh when we speak of *Old*-man," he said. "You should laugh aloud with us when we speak of him. He expects it and always laughs with us from the past."

I have tried to prove for myself that *Old*-man, under different names, is an under-god of all tribes, and as far as I have been able to go, I have found that he is.

The novice, writing of Indian beliefs and customs, is a dangerous man if his findings are to be recorded as historical facts. For after all my study, the Indian is still much of a mystery to me. He has trusted me and has always been willing to tell me of himself, but he is fair and attributes to *you* a mind as great or greater than his *own*. There is the trouble. Ask him: "Is the sun God?" and he may reply "yes" — simply "yes," for he believes that you know that ALL is God. He reasons if you desired further information you would ask for it in a direct question. Therefore, out of respect for you, he volunteers no information — no extra measure. You must know much of the Indian or you will learn nothing directly from him. He is a poor teacher, and your beliefs or findings concerning him are your own, and of no importance to him. He insists that this should be so, for, above all, the Indian is an individualist in all things.

White men who have lived lifetimes with tribes often know almost nothing of the people.

FOREWORD

Men who have tried to learn have sometimes jumped at conclusions concerning the religion and customs of the Indian, and because of direct answers to single direct questions, have recorded untruths. It is far too late to study the Indian, now. The old men are dead. The young men have learned little of their ancient customs. What we have saved of facts is full of distortions.

Men have called him a stoic — a man without humor, and as such the Indian is branded for all time, I fear. But he is full of humor and feels keenly as do all natural men. He hides his emotions because of his respect for others, and I believe that his silence in the great out-of-doors is because of his reverence for other created things which can neither speak nor move. Created by the same power, he shrinks from flaunting his special favors before them, and so is silent, lest his power to move and speak make them jealous before his god. He believes that to all of His creations the All-wise

FOREWORD

gave some peculiar power, and instead of being jealous of these gifts, which he often recognizes as greater than his own, he respects them as special marks of respect from the hand of his own Maker. Strength, bravery, endurance, speed, and cunning — everything that contributed to make his own wild life a success, or marked him with distinction as an individual among his kind, is reverenced when possessed in an equal or greater degree among the lower animals and birds. He will tell you that the Antelope is swifter, the Bear greater in war, and the Wolf a more cunning hunter than he; and if you beat him at any game he knows, even though he might be the most skillful of his tribe, he will proclaim you as his friend — a greater man than himself. There is no jealousy in his heart, and he is the most graceful loser among men. It is true he will give no voice to his suffering. To do so would give his friends pain and his enemies joy, and he will contribute to neither by his groans.

FOREWORD

He believes in a future life and does not exclude from his heaven other created beings. He does not dare to decide who are fit for his paradise, but leaves that to his god. Because he believes that in a future life there will be happiness and comfort (and in the Indian's life on earth there was hardship and hunger) he has supposed that his dog and his pony will share in that life, and contribute to his welfare as they did in his life on earth. Old Indians have told me that there was no devil "until the black-robes brought him," and so I take it that in the pure beliefs of the Redman there was no such thing as Satan. I have been told by aged Indians that all men, save suicides, go to heaven, eventually, and that all men are punished here for their ill deeds. They say that some do not reach the good land at once, but tarry with the ghost-people in the sand-hills. After a time, however, these go to heaven with the rest.

Nearly seventy years ago a band of Chippe-

was, several hundred strong, disliking the en-
croachments of the white men, came to the
plains to stay. Their wars with the Sioux,
and the fact that they had, at the beginning of
the eighteenth century, driven them from the
Lake Superior district to the Dakotas, would
seem to prove that the Chippewas had always
used the plains at will, although essentially a
forest tribe. This band of Chippewas, upon
leaving the main tribe to the eastward, associ-
ated themselves with the Crees, with whom
the Chippewa nation claims kinship, and thus
became involved in the Riel Rebellion in
1885.

Even though surrounded by mists of super-
stition there is yet beauty in the rites and ceremonies of the Indian. Dignity is always present. I was in the lodge of Big Rock, a medicine-
man of the band of Chippewas (by adoption I
am his brother), when I took part in a "medi-
cine-smoke." Charles Russell, the cowboy artist, has made a drawing of the setting within

the lodge, as described by me at the time, and it is herewith appended. In the ceremony will be found much of the religion of these people. I believe it covers all of the essential points, and I will therefore describe it.

The lodge was on the plains, and, as is usual, a rawhide guy-rope reached from the top of the lodge-poles to the ground inside the lodge, where it was fastened to a stake. Before beginning the ceremony this was removed because "we are not afraid of the winds when we smoke the medicine-pipe," explained Big Rock, and "besides the rope divides us in the lodge. It comes between men." An imaginary trail led straight across the lodge from west to east. It was not occupied nor littered. It was the open way for the spirits of all departed beings, and was spoken of as the "Buffalo's trail." A painted lodge is a constantly offered prayer, and as it must face the East, the imaginary trail is also the way of the sun. Sometimes painted lodges among other tribes face

the South, that the sun, at his meridian height, may look through the door; but the lodges of the medicine-men that I have known face the East. The first fire in the imaginary trail was the Sacred fire — the Holy fire, and was but four glowing coals that had been taken from the regular lodge-fire and deposited in a square within a square of the perfectly cleaned earth. Each spear of grass and foreign thing was carefully removed before the coals were deposited, and only sweet-grass or sweet-sage was burned upon the coals. In the smoke of the incense given off by the fuel, the pipe-bowls, stems, and even the hands of the company were cleansed at the beginning of the ceremony. On either side of the imaginary trail and opposite the Holy fire knelt a brave. The one on the right, looking east, was the pipe-man, and the other was the keeper of the Holy fire. At the beginning of the ceremony four wooden images of men were set at the head of the imaginary trail, at the west, and in front of each was a pipe, its bowl resting on the ground in the trail, its stem supported by a forked stick that was stuck in the ground. In front of the pipes toward the fire was the skull of a buffalo-bull, and in front of that the claws of a grizzly bear. Next, in front of the claws, was the Holy fire, and between that and the lodge-fire were two stones touching each other, one representing Big Rock and the other myself. (I asked why they were there, and he said we were "One like the other.") The four images, collectively, represent Manitou. They also represent his great lieutenants — his "helpers," which are the sun, the father, the earth, the mother; the moon and the stars, the four seasons; and the north, east, south, and west winds.

There was silence for a few minutes now. No one moved, but all gazed at the Holy fire. All were kneeling in Indian fashion. Then the pipe-man filled a pipe, handed him by Big Rock, while the keeper of the Holy fire laid sweet-grass upon the coals. When the smoke of the sweet-grass ascended, the pipe-man lighted the pipe and gravely passed it to Big Rock. Solemnly the old warrior rose to his knees and offering the stem of the pipe to the sun, prayed for life: "Oh, Father, make us to pity each other," trembled from his lips as he finished. Then he turned the pipe-stem to the earth and his prayer was almost the same as that offered to the sun, only he addressed himself to "Mother." After these invocations the pipe was proffered to the four winds, the four seasons — the four points of the compass, and there was little variation in any of the prayers, save that he implored the winds to be kind. Never have I heard such fervor — such intense feeling as his voice expressed. It shook with reverence and awe. When the prayers were finished, Big Rock smoked, inhaling four deep draughts from the pipe; when he passed it — as the sun goes — about the lodge, and the stem was always care-fully pointed toward the lodge-wall in its passing. With these people the pipe may, and did, pass the doorway, which is forbidden by the Blackfeet. Each of the four pipes were sent around the lodge, much as the first had gone, save that when the last one was taken up, Big Rock addressed the "Three Chief Stars" in prayer, ere he passed it to the others. If a pipe went out or was emptied, it was returned by the same route it had travelled, always with care that the stem pointed to the lodge-wall. It came back to the hands of Big Rock, and by him was handed to the pipe-man, when it was refilled, lighted, and passed back to begin its round where it had left off.

I have asked old Indians "what becomes of all the animals that have been slain since the world began?" and I have had them face the South and move the hands in a circle, as the sun goes, leading me to believe that "nothing is destroyed," was the answer intended. The Indian is intensely religious and profoundly superstitious; but the reasons for some of his most

FOREWORD

solemn ceremonies have been lost. Even the words of ancient songs are lost, and he uses words he cannot define, he has told me.

It is a mistake to declare that the Indian does this or that. Tribes differ materially in customs, and while I have been led to believe that, fundamentally, their religion is much the same, they do not agree in all particulars. But, unlike ourselves, they declare each man to be right in his own beliefs, and would have him hold fast to them without intruding their own.

FRANK B. LINDERMAN.

CONTENTS

QUO–TOO–QUAT

QUO–TOO–QUAT

WAR EAGLE, the old Medicine Man, sat in his great painted lodge with his grandchildren. The fire had burned low, and his stern face was softened in the dim, yellow light. The wind rustled in the rose bushes nearby, and the sound of the waters of the Marias — the River That Scolds at the Other — came to the lodge with it. The night was dark and the stars were behind heavy clouds. War Eagle laid aside his pipe.

"Tell us a story, grandfather," said Eyes-in-the-water. "Tell us of *Old*-man. We like to hear about him. He was such a funny person." And she laughed.

War Eagle stirred the fire until it burned brightly. "Now I can see you better. My eyes are growing old," he said, and smiled.

3

"If you will promise to go to your beds when I have finished, I will tell you the story of Quo-too-quat, the Cripple."

"We promise," they said.

"That is good," said War Eagle. "It was long ago — oh, ever so long ago that it happened. It was even before my grandfather lived.

"Two girls were picking flowers in the forest. It was in the month of roses and the day was bright with sunshine. The girls were sisters and were both beautiful. Red Wing was the older, and when they had wandered far from the camp, she said to her sister: 'Let us go on until the night comes, and then we will sleep in the silence, just you and I. It will be fine to hear the night birds call to each other, and watch the Dark creep upon the world from its hiding place. I know its den must be near, for it runs away each day before the Sun comes, and as soon as he goes to his lodge in the West the Dark comes back again. Let us stay in

4

the forest and watch. Perhaps we shall learn where the Dark hides in daytime.'

"'I am afraid,' said Laughs-in-the-morning. 'I am afraid, sister. There are bears and gray wolves in the forests. Why do you want to do such a thing?'

"'I have told you, Laughs-in-the-morning. I would watch the Dark creep from its den. I would learn its secret,' said Red Wing. 'Do this for me. Let us sleep in the great forest this one night.'

"They went on, picking a flower here and there, until the Sun had gone. Then the little Shadows began to creep out of the bushes. 'The Dark will soon be here,' they whispered before they went away. And then the big Shadows came out of the brush. They crept from tree to tree and watched Red Wing and Laughs-in-the-morning make their bed of boughs. 'The Dark is coming,' they said, even louder than the little Shadows had spoken, but the girls did not hear them. Before they knew

5

what was happening the Dark had come, and so silently, so cunningly that they could not even tell the direction from which it came.

"Soon those things that see best in the Dark began to travel about the forest. Most of these are warlike things that live upon those who sleep at night — wolves and cougars and foxes and owls. Some are great, while others are small, but all live by killing those things that work and walk in the sunshine. It was always so. Bad things love the Dark.

"Then, finally, the Stars came and looked down at Red Wing and Laughs-in-the-morning. 'Stars are beautiful,' said Red Wing. 'Wouldn't it be wonderful if we could have husbands that were like the stars. Let us each pick out a star and pretend they are our husbands. I see mine now. It is that bright one just over the top of that pine-tree.'

"'And mine is that star that is shining and twinkling over the dead top of that fir-tree,' said Laughs-in-the-morning. 'I am going to

6

call him Eagle. I think that is a beautiful name, don't you, sister?'

"'Yes, I do. But I shall call my husband Night Sun,' said Red Wing. 'Let us talk to our husbands without speaking aloud.' And they did.

"Owls called in the forest, and wolves came close to the bed of boughs. Once a red fox walked right up to the bed, but the girls did not see him. He looked, and then went away.

"'Come and take me up to your world, Eagle,' said Laughs-in-the-morning. She did not speak aloud, but she looked at the Star and thought the words.

"'Come and get me, Night Sun,' said Red Wing to her Star. But she only thought the words, which is the same as speaking them.

"'Where are we, sister? What is this bright light?' It was Laughs-in-the-morning that spoke. 'Oh, where are we?'

"Red Wing sat up and covered her eyes with her hand. The light was brighter than the

7

Sun and was all about them. 'I do not know,' she said. 'What is that? — Why, it is an old woman. See, she is watching us. Let us ask her where we are. Old Woman, tell us where we are, and what this light is that blinds us.'

"The Old Woman was sitting on a cloud nearby, and she said: 'Young women, this is not your country. Some Stars have brought you here, but you must not stay. They are all sleeping now, but will soon awake. Come with me. I will help you. I know who you are. I am related to your mother. Those Stars must not find you here. Come.'

"She hopped off the cloud and went into a lodge that was near. It was her own lodge; and she brought out a rope of twisted bark and a bag that had been made of the white skins of some strange animals. She tied one end of the bark-rope to the bag. 'Get into the bag,' she said.

"The girls did as she told them, and then the

8

Old Woman said: 'This is a Medicine Rope and has no end but the one I have tied to the bag. Do not be afraid but keep saying *Quo-too-quat*, *Quo-too-quat*, *Quo-too-quat*, until you are in your own country. Good-by. I shall never see you again.'

"She raised a door in the sky and let the bag down, down, down, until it came to this world. It was in the forest some place where the bag touched the world. The girls got out, and Flash! the bag was gone. The air smelled as it does when the Thunder speaks sharply, and the girls were alone in the wilderness again.

"'What shall we do, Red Wing? I am very hungry,' said Laughs-in-the-morning.

"'I do not know, sister, but let us travel. Perhaps we shall find some people who will give us food.'

"The day was fine. They began to look for food. They came to where camas grew, and they dug much and ate it.

"'Is that a lodge yonder?' asked Laughs-in-the-morning. 'It looks like a lodge. Let us go and see.'

"'I am so tired,' said Red Wing. 'You go and see if it is a lodge, and I will wait here for you to come back.'

"But Laughs-in-the-morning did not come back. She grew bewildered and could not find her way. Red Wing set out to find her, but could not. They were separated, and they both wandered back into the forest.

"Laughs-in-the-morning saw a man coming through the bushes. She was frightened. The man had only one leg. It was Quo-too-quat, the Cripple. She had heard of him. He was a great hunter. Her grandfather had told her that. Quo-too-quat knew magic, and so she was afraid of him. He began to laugh as he came near, and Laughs-in-the-morning cried.

"'Tell me who is troubling you and I will kill him,' said Quo-too-quat, the Cripple. His voice was rough, but his eyes looked kind.

"'My sister is lost. Oh, I cannot find her!

10

Red Wing has wandered away,' said Laughs-in-the-morning.

"'Ho! Well I know where she is, of course. Come, and I will take you to her.'

"He began to hobble away through the forest. Laughs-in-the-morning followed as fast as she could, for Quo-too-quat, the Cripple, walked rapidly with a magic stick. Laughs-in-the-morning was growing tired when Quo-too-quat stopped to talk to a gray wolf in the bushes.

"'Brother,' said Quo-too-quat to the Wolf, 'have you seen the White Buffalo lately?'

"'Yes,' said the Wolf. 'They are near the foot of the Big Mountains. I saw them yesterday. There are many buffalo with them that are not white.'

"'That is good,' said Quo-too-quat, 'but do not chase the White Buffalo. Tell your people that I said they must not make the White Buffalo run. Remember that. I am going to take this girl to my lodge. Then I will go with you to the Mountains. Wait here for me.'

"Laughs-in-the-morning was glad when she heard Quo-too-quat tell the Wolf that, because she knew that the lodge could not be far away.

"What a queer lodge it was, though! It was made of the leaf fat of buffalo, and every lodge-pole was painted yellow.

"Red Wing was sitting on some robes and sprang up when Quo-too-quat opened the door. 'Oh, Laughs-in-the-morning! I am so happy to see you again, my sister. I thought you would never, never come. Here, sit here and eat. This is the lodge of Quo-too-quat, the Cripple. He brought me here that day when you wandered away. I do not know how long I have been here. How long has it been since you left me?'

"'I do not know, sister,' said Laughs-in-the-morning. 'This is not our country. That Old Woman made a mistake, I fear. What country is this, Quo-too-quat?'

"But Quo-too-quat was gone.

"'He has been good to me, sister,' said Red

12

Wing. 'There is always plenty of meat here, and he treats me well.'

"'I wish we were with our own people, sister,' said Laughs-in-the-morning.

"'Yes, I do, too, but perhaps he will take us there if we ask him.'

"'How! How!' said a squeaky voice at the door. Then a very old and wrinkled face peered inside.

"The girls screamed. They were frightened.

"'Ha, ha, ha!' cackled the man with the wrinkled face. 'Don't you know me? I knew your grandfather and his father and even your grandfather's father. Ha, ha, ha. I am *Old*-man. Don't be afraid of *me*. *Nobody* is afraid of *me*. Ha, ha, ha. What is that?' He pointed to a bone whistle that hung from a lodge-pole over Red Wing's head.

"'That,' said Red Wing, 'is Quo-too-quat's Buffalo Whistle. Whenever he sits on a big rock and blows the Whistle four times, the buffalo come.'

"'Oh, yes. Ha, ha, ha. I only wanted to see if you knew. That is the way I do. I sit on a big rock and blow my whistle four times and the buffalo always come. Lots of them. Ha, ha, ha. But mine is a better whistle than that one. Let me see that whistle.' He took it down from the lodge-pole and said: 'I guess I could make this old thing do. Comb your hair and make yourselves look nice, for we shall have a big feast when I come back. I am going to kill some buffalo. Ha, ha, ha.'

"'Oh!' cried Red Wing. 'Do not take the Whistle of Quo-too-quat.'

"'I will not hurt his whistle. I only want to borrow it. I shall bring it back,' said *Old*-man. And he went away with the Whistle and his bow and arrows.

"After he had gone Laughs-in-the-morning said: 'We had better comb our hair as he told us. I am afraid of *Old*-man. He does wicked things sometimes. Let us comb our hair right away.'

"'I will braid your hair, sister, if you will do mine,' said Red Wing.

"'There! He cannot complain now,' said Laughs-in-the-morning when they had finished.

"*Old*-man found a big rock and sat upon it. Then he began to blow Quo-too-quat's Whistle. One-two-three-four. One-two-three-four.

"He soon heard a deep rumbling sound, and the ground trembled with the weight of many hoofs. 'Ho!' said *Old*-man. 'Ho! there are plenty of buffalo coming. Ha, ha, ha.' He heard the brush crackling and saw a great herd of buffalo tramping toward him. There were two White Buffalo leading the others, straight to the big rock where *Old*-man sat blowing Quo-too-quat's Whistle. When the White Buffalo were close to him, *Old*-man began to shoot his arrows at them as fast as he could; but the arrows broke in pieces. They did not draw blood. Their sharp points broke, and the Buffalo did not fall. They were surprised and angry at *Old*-man, and ran away, taking

15

the great herd with them. He had killed none.

"'That is strange,' he said. 'My arrows did not go through the skin of those White Bulls. I wonder why.'

"He had lied to Red Wing. He had said that he knew about the Buffalo Whistle; that he had one like it, only better. He had no whistle at all. He had never heard of those White Buffalo. They were Medicine Bulls, and of course *his* arrows would not kill them.

"Quo-too-quat heard the Whistle. 'Who can be blowing my Buffalo Whistle?' he said to the Wolf.

"'I don't know, brother, but somebody will make trouble. Those White Bulls are bad when they are angry. You'd better go and see who blew that Whistle,' replied the Gray Wolf.

"Quo-too-quat ran; for his magic stick helped him to travel as fast as other men, and faster. When he got to his lodge, the girls were gone.

"The White Buffalo had carried them away

— the Medicine Bulls had stolen them. They were angry at Quo-too-quat for lending his Whistle and had taken the girls away.

"Quo-too-quat was frightened. He did not know what might happen to Red Wing and Laughs-in-the-morning. He put on his heavy moccasin and took his strongest walking-stick. 'I shall go and find them while they are yet alive,' he said. 'They were good girls, and I am sure they have done nothing that is wrong.'

"Just as he raised the door of his lodge to set out, he saw *Old*-man coming. He was crying. He knew that he had lied, and that something had happened to make Quo-too-quat angry.

"'They told me to blow on your Whistle,' he said, 'and I *did* blow it, but I couldn't kill those White Bulls. My arrows broke, and ——'

"'Oh,' said Quo-too-quat, 'you tried to kill the Medicine Bulls, did you? They are friends of mine. Now I'll teach you manners. Maybe you will tell the truth and mind your own business after this.'

"He began to beat *Old*-man's legs with his bow. 'Ow — oh — ow!' cried *Old*-man as he ran through the woods. But Quo-too-quat was close at his heels and struck him many times. 'Oh — ow — oh! That's enough! That's enough! I'll remember. Oh — ow — oh! I'll tell the truth and mind my own business, Quo-too-quat.'

"Then Quo-too-quat left him and turned to look for the trail of the White Buffalo. He was going to follow it.

"When *Old*-man got far enough away he called: 'I'm glad I did that! I hope you never find those girls. Ha, ha, ha!' He turned and ran. His cackling laugh made the pine squirrels wonder, and the Bluejay said to the Magpie: 'That's *Old*-man. I wonder what he's been doing.'

"'I don't know,' said the Magpie. 'He's pretty mean — meaner than I am, and I'm pretty mean, myself.'

"Quo-too-quat had climbed a high hill. He

18

had left the trail of the White Buffalo because he expected to cut them off by crossing the high hill. There were great pine-trees growing there, and near one of them he saw a White Elk. It was a bull, and he was white as the snow. All those things that are white when their kind is of a different color are Big Medicine. Quo-too-quat called to the White Elk.

"The White Elk came to him, for they all knew him. He was a Big Medicine Man.

"'Have you seen two girls? They were carried away from my lodge this morning,' said Quo-too-quat to the White Elk.

"'Yes, I know where they come to get water, too. I saw them a little while ago. There are two white buffalo bulls with them. You must be careful. Those bulls are bad. I know those bulls. They have wicked hearts.'

"'Show me where I can find them, brother,' said Quo-too-quat. 'My Medicine is strong. We must not wait. I am afraid those White Bulls will kill the girls.'

"'Follow me,' said the White Elk; and he led Quo-too-quat up a mountain and down the other side without once speaking. At the bottom he stopped to listen.

"'Tap-tap-tap — tap-tap-tap-tap.' A woodpecker was hammering upon the dead trunk of a fir-tree.

"'Stand still, Quo-too-quat. Do not move or speak. I 'll see if Woodpecker knows where those girls are now. If he sees you, he will fly away.'

"Quo-too-quat stood very still, and the White Elk walked toward the Woodpecker, pretending to be feeding on the grass as he went so that Woodpecker would not be afraid. When he got close he said:

"'Woodpecker.'

"'Oh! You scared me,' said the Woodpecker. 'What is it you want?'

"'Have you seen two girls to-day?'

"'Yes,' said Woodpecker, 'but don't come any closer. I 'm afraid of you. Those girls are down near that creek. There are two White Buffalo Bulls with them. Be careful.' Then he climbed higher up on the tree and began again: 'Tap-tap-tap-tap-tap.' He was minding his own business.

"The White Elk called to Quo-too-quat and told him what Woodpecker had said. 'I'll wait here, Quo-too-quat. I can't make war on those White Bulls. Be careful. Those Bulls are wicked. Take your time and get very close,' he warned.

"Quo-too-quat crept to the creek and listened. The water made a noise as it rippled over the stones, so he moved a little farther from the bank.

"'Brrrrr,' said one White Bull to the other. 'Brrrrr, let us kill these girls. They are a nuisance and Quo-too-quat lends his Whistle to everybody.'

"'Brrrr,' said the other Bull. 'Brrrr, I am willing. But let us wait until the night comes.'

"It was getting dark even then. Shadows

were coming into the forest so Quo-too-quat knew that the Night was near. He selected two very sharp Medicine arrows. They were painted and there were strange marks upon their shafts. Their feathers were from the left wing of a white goose, and would guide them straight.

"Then Quo-too-quat put the arrows in his mouth and walked like the Bear-people until he came close to the camp of the White Bulls. They were sitting near their fire. Laughs-in-the-morning was crying, and Red Wing was trying to comfort her. The wicked White Bulls were laughing at them, when Zip!— Zip! went the two Medicine arrows from Quo-too-quat's bow.

"'Oh!' said both the White Bulls as they sank to their knees near the fire.

"Quo-too-quat ran to them and pushed the arrows deeper into their wicked hearts with his hands. Then they died.

"'Come, let us go to my lodge,' said Quo-too-quat to the girls. 'You can never go back to your own country now. It is too far away. Besides, your people have moved camp.' Ho!"

WHY OUR SIGHT FAILS WITH AGE

WHY OUR SIGHT FAILS WITH AGE

CHICKADEE'-DEE-DEE-DEE. Chicka-dee-dee-dee-dee.

"Oh, he almost came inside the lodge, grand-father!" cried Bluebird, as a chickadee flew to a bush near the door. "I like the chickadees. They are always so friendly and happy. I pre-tend they are laughing when they are in the willows and rosebushes. They do seem to be laughing, don't they, grandfather?"

"Yes," said War Eagle. "That is what *Old*-man thought one day long ago. It made trouble for us all, too — bad trouble that visits us if we live to be old."

"Tell us the story, grandfather!" cried Buf-falo-Calf. "We will help grandmother gather dry wood if you will tell us about *Old*-man."

"That is good. I will tell you," said War

27

Eagle. "It was in the forest where great trees grew, and where many bushes and vines covered the ground about them. *Old*-man was alone. He had seen no people since morning, and the Sun was already looking toward his lodge in the West. 'Listen,' he said; but he was only talking to himself. 'Listen.' He bent and placed his hand behind his ear, that he might hear better. Ha! somebody was laughing among the trees and bushes. It was not loud laughing, but the Person was having a good time all by himself, whoever it was.

"'That is funny — so much laughing,' said *Old*-man. 'I'll go and see who it is that laughs. I'd like to laugh, myself, if I could find something funny. I have looked, too, and there is nothing to laugh at.'

"He hurried toward the sound of laughing, making so much noise in his travelling that he could not hear the Person laugh. He stopped and listened. Ho! it was gone. The Person had moved. *Old*-man stood very still for a

28

while, and then he heard the laughing again, but it was far away.

"'That is strange,' he said. 'That Person seems to find something that makes him happy wherever he goes. He was here and laughed, but I can see nothing to laugh at. Now he is over near that big tree and is laughing again. I must find that Person.'

"He hurried onward. He even ran; but twice the Person moved with his laugh before he came close to a small tree with thick leaves upon its branches.

"'Chickadee-dee-dee-dee. Chickadee-dee-dee-dee.' Ho! it was the Chickadee laughing.

"'What are you laughing at?' asked *Old*-man. 'I've travelled hard all this day and haven't seen a funny thing.'

"'That makes me laugh,' said the Chickadee. And he did laugh. 'Chickadee-dee-dee-dee!'

"'Are you laughing at me?' cried *Old*-man.

"'No. Oh, no — not exactly,' said the Chickadee. 'But if a Person cannot get along with himself, how can he laugh? Laugh is a prisoner with a cross person.'

"'What were you laughing at before I came?' asked *Old*-man.

"'Watch me,' said the Chickadee.

"Then he took out his eyes and tossed them away up among the branches. The Chickadee sat very still and waited for them to come down again. The eyes came straight back and landed plump! in their places, as if they had not been away. 'Chickadee-dee-dee-dee!' He was laughing again, and that made *Old*-man laugh, too.

"'Ha, ha, ha! That *is* funny. Do it again.'

"'All right. Watch me,' said the Chickadee.

"Up went his eyes a second time, and down they came plump! into their places. And the Chickadee laughed again.

"'Ha-ha, ha! ha, ha, ha! That *is* funny. Show me how to do it, Chickadee,' said *Old*-man.

"'Oh, no — no,' said the Chickadee. 'You cannot do it. You are too clumsy. You can

30

do nothing well, and in trying you might get into trouble.'

"'Please, brother,' begged *Old*-man. 'Tell me the secret. I will be careful. I made you, and you should be good to me.'

"'Yes,' said the Chickadee, 'you made me, but you made a lot of enemies for me, too. I have more than anybody, and they are every-where. No, this is my secret. You would blame me if you tried it and got into trouble.'

"'No, I will never blame you, brother. Tell me the secret and I will give you my necklace. See, it is very handsome.'

"The Chickadee looked at the necklace and became proud. He wanted to wear it. He thought it would make him more beautiful, so he said: 'All right, I'll tell you the secret. Then you must look out for yourself. I don't do·this thing very often, myself, and I'm not clumsy as you are. You take out your eyes and throw them as high as you want them to go. They will always come straight back to

31

their places if you do not move, nor laugh, nor even breathe while they are away. If you do any of these things, your eyes will be lost. Remember that. I have told you what not to do, and if you forget you will have to pay for it. That is all there is to the secret. Now give me that necklace.'

"*Old*-man took off his necklace and gave it to the Chickadee. Then he cried: 'Watch me.' He took out his eyes and tossed them far up among the trees. He stood still — did not laugh — did not move — did not even breathe. Plump! the eyes came back to their places as the Chickadee had said they would. *Old*-man laughed, and the Chickadee laughed with him.

"'Good-by, my brother. I shall have something to laugh at now,' said *Old*-man. And he went away in the forest.

"He tried the Chickadee's trick over and over, laughing each time, and each time tossing his eyes higher, until at last he grew careless. Ho! he moved his head. He laughed. He even

32

breathed before his eyes came back. He was standing in a thickly timbered spot when he tossed his eyes upward. They were gone a long time. He was all ready to laugh, and couldn't wait. He heard something strike the ground near him. Then he was frightened. He was blind. He had no eyes. They had fallen on the ground among the dead leaves and dirt. Ho! *Old*-man was in trouble. Now he did not laugh. He cried. Yes, he cried. Oh ho! now he was sorry that he had met the Chickadee. He got down on his hands and knees and began to feel about for his eyes as one feels for things in the dark. Once he touched a snail and thought it was one of his eyes.

"Then at last he found his eyes in the dirt and leaves where they had fallen. He put them back in their places, but they hurt him because of the dirt that had clung to them while they were upon the ground. He never got over it. No. He could never see so well as he had before he did that foolish thing.

"Of course he made us all pay for his trouble. He always does. When he knew his eyes would never be so good as they were before he met the Chickadee that day, he said:

"'After this there shall come a time in the lives of old people when their eyes shall not be very useful. They shall bother them before they die, as my eyes bother me.' It has been true from that day to this.

"The Chickadee and all his children wear *Old*-man's necklace since that day, and you have seen it about their necks, of course. The necklace is too heavy for a bird so small as the Chickadee, and its weight keeps him from flying very high in the air. He always stays near the ground in the bushes or small trees because of the heavy necklace that *Old*-man gave him that day in the forest. Ho!"

WHY CHILDREN LOSE THEIR TEETH

WHY CHILDREN LOSE THEIR TEETH

THE fire in War Eagle's lodge was burning brightly when the children entered.

There was an air of mystery among them as they seated themselves about the cheerful blaze.

"What would you tell me? I know you have something to say by looking at your faces. I have finished my smoking. You may speak," he said.

Eyes-in-the-water arose and stepping to her grandfather's side she thrust forth her little hand, which, upon reaching its arm's length suddenly opened, exposing a tiny tooth. "See, grandfather. See, I have lost a tooth. It came out of my mouth."

There was awe in the eyes of the children as gravely the old warrior took the tooth from his granddaughter's hand and smiled.

"Six snows have passed," he said. "It does

not seem so long as that since you came to live on this world, Eyes-in-the-water. But it must be so—six snows."

"It's almost seven snows, grandfather," declared Muskrat; "for I am nearly nine, now."

"And did not your teeth fall out, young warrior?" asked War Eagle.

"Yes, but I was not frightened," said the boy. "Everybody loses his teeth, does'nt he, grandfather?"

"Yes," he said. "Oh, yes, and it is all because of *Old*-man. All because he was greedy and dishonest, but we have paid for it all. All the people have paid, and will pay, as long as there are people."

"Tell us about it, grandfather," begged the children.

"Put two sticks upon the fire, Muskrat, and I will tell you how it came about. Of course it was long ago, and in the fall when the leaves of the cottonwoods were yellow along the streams. There was not a cloud in the sky, and the wind had not visited the plains for days. One could see an object a long distance upon the ground or in the air, for the days were clear in the bright sunshine. It was one of those days when echoes sleep lightly and are easily disturbed by travellers.

"*Old*-man was walking toward a hilltop on the plains when he saw a Crane flying over the land. 'That bird is going toward water, I know,' said *Old*-man, for he talks much to himself. 'I 'll watch the Crane and see where he goes. That is what I will do.'

"The Crane flew on until he seemed but a speck in the air. Then he suddenly dropped from sight. He was gone.

"'That is funny,' said *Old*-man. 'I can't see any water where the Crane came to the ground, but I will go and see. That is a wise Person, and perhaps I shall learn something new.'

"He walked fast and at last came to a river. It was not a large stream, but it was very crooked and made great bends as it flowed through the land. The ground was deeply cut by the water, and the river banks were high, and sometimes steep; but trees grew along the stream under the banks in little meadow-places that were pretty to look upon.

"*Old*-man looked for the Crane but could not see him. The water rippled over sand-bars, and was shallow in some places and deep in others, like most of the rivers that flow through the plains, but the Crane was not in sight. He called: 'Hey, you Crane-person! Where are you?' Echoes answered him, and his own voice came back from the banks of the stream and seemed to mock him. That made *Old*-man angry. 'Hey, you Crane-bird!' called *Old*-man, and 'Hey, you Crane-bird!' the echoes answered. 'I want to talk to you, Crane,' yelled *Old*-man, and 'I want to talk to you,' yelled the echoes. Ho! he was growing angrier at every call because the echoes mocked him. 'Don't talk to me, you Echo-people,' he roared, and 'Don't talk to me, you Echo-people,' came

40

back to him from the banks and among the trees. 'I 'll stop talking, myself,' he said, and no words came back to him, for he had not spoken them loudly as he had the others. On he went down the stream when, turning a bend in the river, he saw the Crane on the far side near the bank. The bird was wading in the shallow water and looking for something to eat.

"'Say, you; why don't you answer when you hear a Person call. When I call People I want them to answer me. I guess I know what I want.'

"'I didn't hear you, *Old*-man,' said the Crane. 'This water makes a lot of noise where I am.'

"'What are you doing here, anyhow?' asked *Old*-man.

"'I 'm minding my own business,' said the Crane. 'What are *you* doing here, yourself?'

"'I 'm looking for something to eat, of course! Don't be so cross.'

"'That 's my business here, too,' said the Crane, 'and I 'm not cross. I — there! You

41

made me lose a big fish with your talking. Why do you talk so much?'

"'Ha, ha, ha,' laughed *Old*-man. 'It serves you right for not answering me when I called you. I hope you don't catch a fish all day. Not even a frog. Ha, ha, ha — ha, ha, ha. Good-by.'

"He left the Crane and went on down the river, which turned and twisted so suddenly that sometimes the sun would be looking upon his face, and at other times it shone upon his back. Sometimes the river crossed great stretches where there were no trees at all, but at other times it ran through groves of cotton-woods. Its course was most crooked in these places. The water liked the shade of the trees, and stayed as long as it could without stopping altogether. Often it was but a little way across the bends by land, and ever so far by the water's route. You have seen rivers that were like that. By walking across the necks of land a man can reach a point down the stream quicker than the water can. Yes, and much quicker than anything that is floating on the water. *Old*-man knew all about that, of course, for he made the rivers — made them straight in some places, but crooked in others.

"In one of the bends of the river *Old*-man saw something floating on the water. Whatever it was bobbed along over the ripples, stopped, and often turned around in the eddies, but after a while it always went with the water. It was round. It was almost white, and it floated well and lightly.

"'That's Back-fat,' said *Old*-man. 'I am sure it is Back-fat. It looks fresh and fine. Yes, I know it is Back-fat. Hey, you Ball-thing,' he cried, 'come in here. Come closer to me. I want to talk to you.'

"The river brought it nearer and nearer until finally it was near the shore, and *Old*-man reached and picked it from the water. It felt like Back-fat in his fingers, and its color was the same as that of Fat, but he was not

43

sure; so he asked: 'What's your name, Ball-thing?'

"'You made me, yourself, and you should know my name without asking *me*,' replied the Ball-thing.

"'Yes, I did make you,' said *Old*-man, 'but everything on this world has *two* names; so tell me your name.'

"'My name is One-bite,' said the Ball-thing.

"'Ha! — Well, I'm hungry,' said *Old*-man, and took one big bite from the Ball-thing, for he was sure that it was Back-fat. Then he tossed the Ball-thing back into the water, and it began its journey down the stream at once.

"But the bite tasted good. 'Good-by, Ball-thing,' cried *Old*-man. But just as the Ball-thing went around a bend in the river, he ran like a deer across a neck of land and so came to the water again and far below the Ball-thing that had to go the way of the stream. When he reached the river he waited, for he knew the water would bring the Ball-thing and, of course, it did. As soon as it came into view *Old*-man called: 'Hey, you Ball-thing. Come closer. I want to talk to you.'

"The Ball-thing came close to the shore with the water, and *Old*-man grabbed it. 'What's your name, Ball-thing?' he asked as though he had never seen it before.

"'You made me, and you should know my name without asking *me*,' said the Ball-thing.

"'Yes, I guess I *did* make you, but everything on this world has *two* names, so tell your name.'

"'My name is One-bite,' said the Ball-thing, and *Old*-man took another and larger bite. He wanted to eat it all, but he was afraid because of the Ball-thing's name, you see. So he threw it back into the stream. As soon as it struck the water *Old*-man ran across another bend and waited for the Ball-thing to come along that way. He was laughing now and talking to himself. 'Ha, ha, ha — Oh — Ho! I'll eat it all — one bite at a time, if this river stays crooked enough.' The Ball-thing nearly passed him before he saw it that time; he was so merry that his eyes were filled with tears — laugh-tears. The Ball-thing was a little way past him when he saw it, and he was obliged to run to catch up, but he called to it and it came to the shore as it had done before. He asked the same questions, and the Ball-thing answered as it had done twice before. *Old*-man bit again. He had taken three bites now, and he threw the Ball-thing back upon the water, but there wasn't much left of it—not much. Of course he ran away to meet the Ball-thing again, and to bite it again, but something had happened. Ho! something queer had happened to the Ball-thing — something that *Old*-man did not know about. The Ball-thing had changed itself into a stone that floats. Its color was the same. Its shape was as before, so that *Old*-man did not know there had been a change.

"Very soon the water brought the Ball-thing around the bend where *Old*-man waited, and he called: 'Hey, you Ball-thing, come in here.

I want to talk to you,' and it came, of course. 'What 's your name, Ball-thing?' he asked.

"'You made me and you should know my name without asking *me*,' said the Ball-thing.

"'Yes, I know I made you, but everything on this world has two names; so tell me your name.'

"'One-bite,' said the Ball-thing, and SWOW! *Old*-man bit the Ball-thing that had turned to stone that floats. Oh, Ho! — Oh, Ho! — all those teeth that grow in front were broken off at the gums, and he spat them into his left hand. Blood was running from his mouth, and tears were in his eyes. Oh, Ho! — Oh, Ho! — now there was no laughing. 'That was a mean trick you played, Ball-thing. That was wrong. You are wicked. You should not treat me so. I made you, and you have hurt me and hurt all the other people of my kind, too, for from this day onward — EVERY CHILD THAT LIVES SHALL LOSE ITS TEETH WHEN SIX SNOWS HAVE PASSED ITS HEAD.'

"Then he threw the Ball-thing back into the river and sat down upon a log and cried over his broken teeth like an old woman. That is why our children lose their teeth. It is just as *Old*-man said it would be; and it was because the Ball-thing made a fool of him. Ho!"

HOW THE SKUNK HELPED THE COYOTE

HOW THE SKUNK HELPED THE COYOTE

"OH, grandfather," cried Muskrat, as the children came to War Eagle's lodge; "oh, grandfather, we found a spring of cold water just over that hill, and it tastes bad and smells awful!"

"Yes, I know about that spring," said War Eagle. "I will tell you about it.

"Once, long ago, a Coyote and his Wife lived in that cave that is back of that spring, and the water was sweet. The Coyote was a good hunter, and his Wife was happy and fat. They had many children, and these went away to find their own homes and wives and children, leaving their father and mother in the cave back of the spring. There was no other place so nice to live in as the Coyote's home, and that made some people jealous.

51

"The snows passed and the grass came many times while the Coyote and his Wife lived in the cave near that spring, but one day the Wolf passed that way and saw how happy and comfortable they were. The Wolf did not like to see his small Cousin so well-off, and he tried to trade his home for the Coyote's cave.

"'No,' said the Coyote. 'My Wife and I are happy here. We have had many children, and still have some little ones to look after. We will not trade. We will stay where we are.'

"'You will, will you?' said the Wolf. 'Well, you won't. I want that cave, and, besides that, My Wife wants it, so you'll have to get out.'

"'No, I won't,' said the Coyote. 'I won't move. I've been here a long time. My father owned this cave before me, and it has always been owned by my family. You must hunt for another place. You can't have this cave.'

"When the Coyote said that, the Wolf grabbed him. There was a terrible battle. The ground was scratched, and hair was all over the place, but the Wolf won, of course. The Coyote was crippled. He never got well. He always limped after that fight. He had to leave the cave, and he was old — lots older than his Wife.

"At last he found a new home and commenced to hunt for food for his family. He met the Fox on a hillside, and the Fox said: 'What are you doing so far from your lodge?'

"'I'm not far from my lodge, brother. I have moved. The Wolf has stolen my cave. I fought him as hard as I could. I guess I'll never get well again. I live on top of this hill, now.'

"'That's too bad,' said the Fox. 'The Wolf is a mean Person.'

"'Yes,' said the Coyote, 'he is mean, but some day I'll get even with him.'

"'I hope so,' said the Fox. 'I hope so. Well, I have to be going. Rabbits are scarce, aren't they? Good-by.'

"When the Fox had gone the Coyote began

to think hard. It brought his mind back to his trouble — his talk with the Fox — and he thought hard. 'I 've got to get help. The Wolf is too many for me, alone,' he said to himself.

"Just then a Rabbit ran down the hill, and he chased him into a hole in the ground. He began to dig him out when, WHEW! an awful smell came to him on the wind. 'Ho!' he said, 'that Skunk Person can make even the winds smell bad.' Then he stopped digging and his cunning eyes were half-closed with thinking. 'Ho!' he cried, 'why didn't I think of that before?'

"He left the Rabbit in his hole and set out with his keen nose to the wind that brought the smell of the Skunk Person to him. Carefully he travelled through the weeds and tall grass till his smart nose told him to go slowly and be very gentle. Then, upon turning a patch of willows that grew on the bank of a creek, he saw the Skunk sucking the eggs in the nest of a Blue Grouse.

"'How, brother,' he said.

"'How — How,' said the Skunk Person. 'Don't you come too close to me or I'll fix you so your own wife won't live with you. Remember that. These eggs are mine. I found them, so stay where you are. I don't want any trouble with anybody, myself.'

"'Neither do I, brother,' said the Coyote. 'I have been looking for you. I want you to help me. I have a favor to ask, and I'll be good to you if you grant it.'

"Then he told the Skunk what the Wolf had done — told him how long he had lived in the cave back of that spring, and showed him his crippled leg as proof of the fight. 'If you will help me, brother, whenever I kill a deer, you may eat all you can hold, and I will not quarrel with you or your children.'

"'I don't see how I can help you. You are stronger than I am. I can't fight the Wolf if you can't. How can I help you, I'd like to know? I can't fight that Wolf.'

"'No,' said the Coyote, 'but you can spoil that water in that spring. You can make the whole place smell so bad that the Wolf can't live there. I guess I know how bad you can make things smell. Everybody does. Will you fix that water so the Wolf and his Wife will have to move? Will you do it?'

"'Yes,' said the Skunk, and he *did* do it.

"The Wolf had to leave. Nobody can stay there since. Nobody can drink that water. Nobody wants to try. Ho!"

WHY THE WEASEL IS WHITE

WHY THE WEASEL IS WHITE

"TO-NIGHT I will tell you why the Weasel is white in winter," said War Eagle. "Put two sticks on the fire, Muskrat, and listen:

"The day was dark and gloomy in the forest. Rain had been falling steadily since the sun had gone to his lodge in the West the day before. All the forest-people were camped under the big spruce-trees, where the ground is always dry. Even the Winds were still and rested in their camps. Everything was wet, and the world smelled wet. The people that live in the ground, like the Rabbit and the Mink and the Skunk, were in their lodges with their families. Even the wolves and the other great hunters were at home waiting for the Sun to come to the world again.

"You would not think that a man would be travelling at such a time, but *Old*-man is seldom still. He is always looking for some kind of trouble, and one can find that in any sort of weather. It is plentiful and everywhere, like the grass. *Old*-man was moving about all that time, and so was Win-to-coo, the Man-eating Person.

"*Old*-man was slipping through a dark cedar swamp where the giant trees made so many shadows that the grass did not grow. Rain dripped through the boughs, and there were pools of water in the holes left by trees that had been uprooted by the winds. He was wet and cold, and was thinking about building a fire, when he saw something moving like a shadow among the trees. It was not a shadow, of course, for shadows do not live without the Sun or the Moon. He stopped and watched until he saw it again. It was a Person — a Bad Person. It was Win-to-coo, the Man-eater, and *Old*-man saw him creep behind a big tree.

"Ho! *Old*-man turned and ran as fast as he could go, for he knew all about the Man-eater. He made that Person, himself, you see, and knew he was wicked. He was afraid of him and ran away.

"Win-to-coo was cunning and pretended that he had not seen *Old*-man. From behind a tree where he had stopped he peeped and watched him run away and hide in some willows that grew near a creek that flowed through the forest. When *Old*-man had hidden himself, Win-to-coo started out in another direction, making believe that he had not seen *Old*-man hide. But when he got far enough to fool him, he turned and began to travel in a circle until he came to the willows. He walked softly. He knew just where to look. *Old*-man, believing that Win-to-coo had not seen him, was just crawling from his hiding-place when Swow! the Man-eater grabbed him by the hair. 'I 've got you! I 've got you, you ——'

"'How! How! my brother,' cried *Old*-man.

'I 'm glad to see you. I 've been looking for you all day.'

"'Ho!' said Win-to-coo, 'there 's no brother of yours here. So you 've been looking for me all day, have you? Liar! Forked-tongue! Cheat! Why did you run out of the cedar swamp when you saw me? Tell me that!'

"'I saw the Bear and I — I didn't want him to know I was there,' lied *Old*-man. 'I didn't see you, Win-to-coo. I didn't even know you were in this country. Let go of my hair. You 're hurting me.'

"'You didn't see me,' laughed Win-to-coo. 'But you saw the Bear. Well, I was there, and I didn't see the Bear, but I saw you. And *now* you see me, don't you? Say! don't you see me *now?*'

"'Yes, yes, I see you now,' said *Old*-man. 'Of course I see you *now*.'

"'Well, that is good, because you will never see me again. I 'm going to roast and eat you. I am hungry. Everything hides when it rains so long.'

"*Old*-man began to cry. 'Do not eat me, Win-to-coo. Do not kill the man that made you.'

"'Yes, you made me,' said Win-to-coo, 'and you told me what to do, and I have always done that. Go now and find dry wood under the spruce-trees. Gather a lot of it and pile it up. I want to build a roasting fire to cook you. Don't you try to run away from me. If you do, I will make you hurt longer. Remember that.'

"*Old*-man knew that he could not run away from Win-to-coo. He had made the Man-eater himself, and knew that he could not beat him running. So he began to gather the wood, begging for his life as he worked. 'This wood is all wet. It won't burn, Win-to-coo. Let me go away. Oh, let me go, Win-to-coo.'

"'Hurry with that wood. You made me and told me how to live,' said the Man-eater. 'Hurry, or I 'll ——'

"'I 'll hurry, Win-to-coo. I 'll hurry. Do not kill me until I get the wood,' begged *Old*-

man. He worked slowly, whining over every stick, but at last he had gathered a pile of dry sticks.

"'That's enough,' said Win-to-coo. 'Now go and cut a long, strong roasting-stick. Get a good one that will hold you, and not let you drop into the fire.'

"Win-to-coo began to build the fire, and *Old*-man watched him until he saw the blaze creep up through the smaller sticks. Then he began to look for the long, strong roasting-stick. He examined many that were good ones, but he pretended that they would not do. He was stealing time. That was what he was doing. He was looking for some one to help him, and kept calling for helpers in a low voice as he walked about the bushes.

"Win-to-coo's fire had burned up grandly, and he sat beside it, warming his hands. The blaze made him sleepy. His eyelids drooped, opened, drooped again — and he was asleep by his fire.

"*Old*-man saw that the Man-eater was asleep, but he dared not try to run away. When he thought of running, his knees grew weak with fright. He kept pretending to look for the roasting-stick and calling for helpers.

"Just as he leaned over a bush to reach for a stick, a Weasel that had come out of his lodge to see how the weather was, spoke to him:

"'How, *Old*-man,' said the Weasel. 'What are you looking for? Why don't you stay in your lodge when it rains?'

"'Oh, my little brother!' cried *Old*-man. 'Oh, brother, I am in trouble. If you will help me, I will do you a favor. I have made the other people handsome, and I will do the same for you if you will help me now. I 'll make you change your robe with the seasons — make each robe to look like the country you live in.'

"'What 's the matter?' asked the Weasel.

"'Look over there by that fire. That is Win-to-coo, the Man-eater. He is going to roast and eat me. I am looking for a roasting-stick for him. I am afraid to run away. He is swifter than I am. I know that, for I made that Person, myself.'

"'I will see what I can do,' said the Weasel. 'You stand still. Do not make a noise. Do not call for helpers, but wait until I return.'

"The Weasel moves quickly and quietly, you know, and he went close to Win-to-coo at the fire. The Man-eater was fast asleep. His mouth was open and his snoring shook the ground. Each breath that came from the huge body stirred the fur upon the Weasel's back as the wind moves the grass upon the ground, but the Weasel is brave. He smiled and stepped backward to get a good start, that he might pass Win-to-coo's teeth before he waked. Then, Swow! he ran down the great throat of that wicked Person. Yes, and when once inside, there was nothing that could stop his work — nothing at all. The Weasel is a great warrior and knows where to strike. He ate Win-to-coo's heart, and of course the Man-eater died.

"When the Weasel came out, he said to *Old*-man: 'Well, that Person is dead. Now do as you promised. Do something for me.'

"'Ho, brave warrior,' said *Old*-man, 'I will do as I promised.' Then he sang:

"'Oh, Weasel, my Brother, Great Warrior;
You shall have but few enemies.
Even these shall not see you.
Swift as the shadows I have made you.
Fat shall always be upon your body;
You have saved me from Win-to-coo.'"

"When he had finished singing he said: 'I give you a white robe for use when the snows come. No snow shall be whiter than you are. But the tip of your tail shall be black to mark you from the other things that are white in winter. I also give you a yellowish-brown robe to wear in the summertime. In this robe you will look like the dead trees and logs that lie upon the ground. You will always be hard to see in any season. This will be good for you and bad for your enemies.'

"That is why the Weasel is brown in summer and white in the winter time. Ho!"

OLD-MAN AND HIS NEW WEAPONS

OLD-MAN AND HIS NEW WEAPONS

THE village had moved and now War Eagle's lodge stood near the edge of a mountain lake. Deer came to drink of the water there in the early morning, or after the sun had gone in the evening. Their trails led far back into the dark forest from the shores of the lake, and the children often followed the well-beaten ways for miles. Flowers grew plentifully, too, for the summer was young, and the shade of the trees was a treat after the sojourn upon the open plains.

A breeze was blowing and the lodge-skins had been raised from the ground. There were no fires burning, and in the gathering twilight the children sat watching their grandfather smoke his pipe. When he had finished and laid it away they begged for a story. War Eagle smiled. "It is well that my memory is good.

If it were poor I could not tell you these stories of long ago, but Manitou is kind. Listen.

"*Old*-man made everything that is on the world. I have often told you that, but sometimes he forgot the names of the things he had made. He often thought they were other than they were, for his memory was poor. Of course he was very old — older than anybody or anything on the world, and memory will not last forever.

"It was early in the summer and in a timbered country where there were many lakes like this one that is near the lodge. *Old*-man had been unlucky in hunting. His arrows were not well made, and so he was hungry much of the time. He sat down on a log and thought of his troubles. Then he spoke to himself: 'If I could find something better with which to make arrow-points, I could do better work. I will look for it. Bone is hard to work into arrow points, and besides I lose so many in hunting. What I want is something that works easily—that's it.'

"He arose and began to search for something with which to make his arrow points. He had not gone far when he came to a pile of black stuff upon the ground near a lake. When the water was high in the lake it covered the black stuff, but it was low now, and the stuff was in plain sight. He picked a piece from the pile. It was heavy and felt hard. 'Ho!' he cried, 'I have found just what I want, and there is plenty of it, too.'

"He sat down near the pile and began to work. He was surprised at the ease with which he could make the black stuff into arrow points, and he made many. They were well made, too, and he fitted them to good shafts, and soon filled his quiver with fine-looking arrows. Then he made a knife from a large piece of the black stuff, and stuck the knife in his belt. He began to laugh then, and talk to himself. 'Ha, ha, ha, I know what I will do. Why didn't I think of it before? I will make two more knives and fasten them to the ends of my bow. That is what I will do. Ha, ha, ha — that will give me more weapons than any other man carries. That will make me a great warrior — greater than any that lives. Ha, ha, ha, why didn't I think of that before, ha, ha, ha.'

"It did not take him long to make the knives and tie them to the ends of his bow. He was pleased with himself, and having many new weapons he set out to look for trouble. New weapons are apt to get us all into trouble. It has always been so. It will be so as long as men live. *Old*-man began to sing his war-song, and when he had finished called out: 'Hey, Bear! I want to fight you. Come where I can see you! Hey, Bear! You are a coward! Don't you hear me calling you? I am at war with you, Bear!'

"Nothing answered except the echoes, but *Old*-man kept travelling and calling; for his new weapons had made him foolish. He was growing warm from fast walking and calling when, at last, he saw the Bear on the far side of a lake.

74

"The Bear was minding his own business, and was digging roots to eat. He had heard no calling because he was busy. When people are busy they do not look for trouble, and it seldom comes to them that mind their own business.

"*Old*-man hid himself behind a dead tree on the ground near the lake. Then he raised himself a little and called: 'Hey, you Humped-up Person over there! You are homely!' Then he hid himself again.

"The Bear stopped his work. His nose was covered with dirt. He looked across the lake but there was nobody in sight. He stood still and listened, but heard nothing but the wind in the tree-tops. 'I guess I must have been mistaken,' he said to himself, and commenced to dig roots again.

"'Hey, you Stub-tail Person over there! What became of your tail?' yelled *Old*-man from behind the tree on the ground.

"The Bear didn't like that talk. Almost

everybody knew how he had lost his tail, and he didn't want people to talk about it. He stopped digging and turned clear around from his work to see who was calling him names, but he didn't see anybody. 'I 'd like to know who that was that called me names,' said the Bear. 'No Person can call me such names. They know better. It 's some foolish one, I guess,' and he turned to his work once more.

"'Here I am, you big coward. I have been looking for you all day. Why don't you come close when I call you. When a Person wants to fight you, do you hide? I want to fight. That is the reason I have been looking for you so long.' *Old*-man stood up so the Bear could see him, and laughed, 'Ha, ha, ha.'

"'You wait right there,' called the Bear. 'You stay right where you are. I 'll come close enough to suit you. I suppose you want to see me get wet, and then run away; but you will have to run far for I shall chase you until we fight. You have made me angry, *Old*-man.'

He plunged into the lake and began to swim across.

"'Ha, ha, ha,' laughed *Old*-man. 'You awkward Person. You Stub-tail Thing. You Humped-up big Fool. Come on! I'm tired travelling and calling to you. I'm tired waiting. You swim slow. Hurry! I want to show you some new weapons,' and he danced on the shore of the lake calling the Bear more names; wasting the breath he would need, in boasting.

"He did not wait for the Bear to reach the land. Oh, no. He was not fair; but as soon as the Bear had come close enough, one, two, three, four, went his arrows. Ho! but they broke. Their points crumbled without making the Bear's blood run.

"'Ho! Come on! Come right along, Bear,' called *Old*-man. 'I have more weapons.' He began to stab the Bear with the knives that were tied to the ends of his bow, but they broke into bits and fell to the ground like willow leaves when the summer is dead.

"'Ha, ha, ha! That is nothing,' he cried. 'I have a big knife yet. Come on, Bear!' But his knife was as poor as his arrows and broke into bits.

"What do you think he had used to make his weapons? Bark — water-logged bark, and he thought it was stone.

"Ho! Now it was the Bear's turn, and *Old*-man fled. The Bear was close to his heels when he dodged behind a clump of willows to run about it. 'Round and 'round they ran. Faster and faster they circled the clump of willows in a mad race. So many times they ran around the clump of willows that the ground was made dusty with their footsteps. There was nothing funny about it now that *Old*-man could see; but he kept at work running. He could not cry nor beg because he needed his breath. It was all he could do to keep his heels from the Bear. They were both breathing hard. The Bear's nose almost touched *Old*-man's moccasins when *Old*-man's toe struck against something

78

and nearly tripped him. He did not know what it was, but his toe gave him pain because of the thing that had struck it. He watched for the thing when he came around the willows again, and what do you think it was? — a buffalo horn that had been there so long that the ground had covered it. When *Old*-man saw what it was he kicked it every time he came to it in his running. He was nearly out of breath when the horn came out of the ground. He was going so fast he couldn't stop, but he slowed down a little bit, and the next time he came to the horn he stooped and grabbed it — stuck it on his forehead and turned upon the Bear. 'Wooh — wooh!' he cried. So suddenly did he turn upon the Bear, and so fierce were the snorts — 'Wooh — Wooh!' that the Bear turned and fled with *Old*-man close behind him snorting 'Wooh — wooh' at every jump and as loudly as his breath would let him.

"The Bear made a great noise in the brush as he ran away, but *Old*-man followed him only a little way. Then he sat down on a log and laughed and laughed — 'Ha, ha, ha — Ho! ha, ha, ha! Oh, Ho! I wonder how many buffalo the Bear thought were after him?'

"Ho!"

LOOKS AT THE STARS

LOOKS AT THE STARS

"STRANGE things happened to men when the world was young," said War Eagle, as he laid aside his pipe. "Put wood on the fire, Buffalo-calf, and I will tell you a story. It has been many snows since it came to my mind.

"Looks-at-the-stars was young, and the world was not old. Our people were camped near the shore of the Big-water, eastward. One night in his father's lodge the Wind spoke to Looks-at-the-stars: 'Come to the Big-water,' it whispered. The young man heard the words of the Wind but he was sleepy and did not heed them. At first the voice of the Wind was low, but it grew louder and louder until it cried: 'Come! Come to the Big-water, Looks-at-the-stars — come to the Big-water!' It shook the lodge. It screamed. It cried out: 'Come to the Big-water, Young-man.' All the sleepers sat up in their beds in the dark, but they saw nothing — heard nothing, save the Wind in the trees. Then the Wind whispered so soft and low that none of the others heard the words: 'Come to the Big-water, Looks-at-the-stars.' When it had whispered, the Wind went away and hid in the bushes near the lodge. Looks-at-the-stars knew it was watching.

"The night was still again. The people in the lodge lay down to sleep once more — all but Looks-at-the-stars. As soon as he was sure that his father was asleep, he took his bow and quiver of arrows and crept out of the lodge. He went to the shore of the Big-water as the Wind had commanded.

"It was smooth, and still as the places where the dead are buried. No waves broke upon the shore. No night-birds spoke from the dark forest behind his father's lodge. Even the Echoes slept soundly in their beds that no man sees. The Moon and the Stars, wife and children of the Sun, looked down at the Big-water from the sky and saw themselves upon it in the night.

"'I am here, Oh, Wind,' whispered Looks-at-the-stars. 'Where are you? What would you have me do?' No one answered. A loon laughed from out on the Big-water where the stars lay thickest upon it. The laugh was like that of ghosts, but Looks-at-the-stars knew that it was the Spotted Loon that laughed, for he knew his voice.

"'I am here, Oh, Wind,' the Young-man whispered, and then he saw a dark object coming toward him from out on the Big-water. It was a birch-bark canoe. The Wind was bringing it out of the night. The canoe was strange and had been made by *other* people in another world. Only the Wind was paddling. The canoe touched the shore at the feet of Looks-at-the-stars and the Wind arose and spoke: 'Get into the canoe, Oh, Young-man. Be not afraid.'

"Looks-at-the-stars knelt in the canoe but

saw no paddle, and he wondered. Then the
Wind sang a song and the canoe left the shore,
paddled only by the Wind. Louder and louder
the Wind sang, and faster and faster the canoe
sped out upon the dark Big-water among the
stars that fled before it. Never before did a
canoe travel so fast. Great waves came from
their lodges when the Wind sang loud, and they
spattered Looks-at-the-stars with their spray,
but he was not afraid. The Moon had hidden
away. The Stars had faded before the graying
light.

"At last the night was driven away by the
Sun, and yet the canoe, paddled by the Wind,
went on. Looks-at-the-stars glanced backward.
The land was gone. He could not see it. Only
the Big-water was near, and it was angry at the
Wind for bringing the canoe, but the Wind was
not afraid and drove the Waves before it. On
and on the Wind paddled the canoe until the
Sun had gone to his lodge in the West and the
Dark was coming fast. 'Boom, boom, boom.'

A great noise was ahead of the canoe and rose above the battle of the Wind with the Waves. The noise came from the foot of a cliff of rocks where the Waves were being driven against it by the Wind. All about the cliff the water was white as the snows of winter, and the Wind shrieked in anger there. Suddenly the canoe was turned, and just as the night drove the light of day from the world of Big-water, it was dashed upon the rocks of a strange land, and broken into pieces.

"The Wind screamed at the Waves as they tore the canoe into bits and threw Looks-at-the-stars high upon the shore. His head struck a rock upon the beach, and the Wind went away with the Waves and left him there. The rock had made him sleep — made him as one who is without power to move throughout the night.

"The Sun of another day was high when Looks-at-the-stars sat up. The Big-water was still. The Wind had gone away. His bow was gone, but the quiver of arrows was still at his shoulder. He rubbed his eyes. He thought he had been dreaming. Suddenly he saw a shadow that moved upon the shore. He turned to see what had made the shadow that moved. Ho! a Mighty Person — a Terrible Person stood near him. So tall was he that he could reach the nests of birds in the tallest tree-tops. His face was covered with hair, and his eyes were blue as the sky in summer. Ho! Looks-at-the-stars was frightened. He sprang to his feet and ran away — ran as the deer runs, along the shore of the strange land. All the day he ran, and fear made his steps long and fast. His breath was gone. His heart was beating like a war-drum when he thought he was far away from the Terrible Person. He thought he was safe and stopped running. There — right before him — he saw the pieces of his own canoe upon the shore. There — right before him — stood the Terrible Person, just where he had left him when he began to run away. Ho! the land was an island! Looks-at-the-stars had run around it. Yes, the strange land was an island, and it belonged to the Terrible Person. He could not escape. He sank to his knees for he was weak from running, and his fear was great. He covered his face with his hands. He was sure that the Terrible Person would take his life.

"'Why did you run away, Young-man?' It was the Terrible Person that spoke. His voice made the ground tremble.

"'I was afraid, oh, Terrible Person,' said Looks-at-the-stars.

"'Why did you come here, Young-man?'

"'The Wind brought me, oh, Terrible Person. I do not lie.'

"'The Wind is my friend,' said the Terrible Person, and he stooped and picked Looks-at-the-stars from the ground as a woman lifts a baby. He swung the Young-man upon his shoulder and set out toward the middle of the island with steps that made the island shake and tremble. The head of Looks-at-the-stars was high above the tallest pine-trees, and he held on by grabbing a braid of the Terrible Person's hair. They travelled in this way until they came to a mountain with a Great Hole in its side, and there was smoke coming from its top. Before entering the Great Hole the Terrible Person lifted Looks-at-the-stars from his shoulder and carried him in his arms, as a woman carries a baby. The Great Hole in the mountain was dark, and as they entered Looks-at-the-stars saw the eyes of many Bears and Wolves staring at him as they passed. The Terrible Person had to stoop as he travelled, and the Dark grew blacker as they entered the mountain. The footsteps of the Terrible Person made a noise like the beating of war-drums as he travelled. Little stones that were moved by his feet rolled away with strange sounds into blacker dark.

"The Young-man looked backward. The Great Hole in the mountain was so far away that it seemed no larger than a man's hand. It looked white in the dark, but the Terrible

Person turned in his course, and it was gone —
gone. All was damp. Water dripped from the
top and sides of the Great Hole in the mountain, and Looks-at-the-stars heard things pass
near them — heard them breathing — saw their
eyes burning like small fires in the night. He
was much afraid and was trembling when he
heard *little voices* singing just ahead. Suddenly
they came to a fire. The smoke and sparks
went straight up through a hole in the top of
the mountain, and about the fire sat many
singers. They had large heads and fierce faces,
but their bodies were bony and small. They
were no larger than little children, and their
chief was a Great Horned Owl.

"They were the Ghost People, of course, and
they lived in that mountain, but when the
Terrible Person stopped by the fire the singers
went away. Where they had been there was
nothing at all — nothing. It was as though
they had never been there.

"'This is my lodge,' said the Terrible Person.

'Let us eat.' He handed Looks-at-the-stars a piece of roasted meat, but it was so heavy that he could not lift it from the ground. He knelt beside the meat and tried to eat, but the meat was so tough he could not chew it. Then he saw the marrow in a bone in the meat, and he began to eat of the marrow. He was very hungry and ate much — so much did he eat that he crawled inside the bone to eat the marrow. When he could eat no more he went to sleep inside the bone and could not tell how long he slept.

"'Young-man — Young-man,' called the Terrible Person. 'Come, I will take you to your people now, but you must never tell them where I live. I do not want visitors. I have no woman. I have no daughters for your young men. I have no sons for your young women, and I have nothing to trade. Remember what I have said. Come.'

"He carried Looks-at-the-stars to the shore of the island near the spot where the canoe had been broken by the waves, and, after making him sit upon his mighty head, the Terrible Person stepped into the Big-water. The Sun was not high in the morning when he began to walk in the Big-water. The water was hardly over his moccasins when the day was half gone, but as the Sun turned toward his lodge in the West the Big-water covered the knees of the Terrible Person, and when the Sun had gone, the Big-water was above his waist.

"The dark came and the Big-water grew deeper, but the Terrible Person kept travelling throughout the night. When morning came again the Big-water was upon the shoulders of the Terrible Person and the feet of Looks-at-the-stars were wet. Little Waves dashed in the face of the Terrible Person when he stopped walking in the Big-water, and said: 'Can you see your own country, now?'

"'I can see the land,' answered Looks-at-the-stars.

"'Well, that is your own country,' said the

Terrible Person. 'It is not far off, now, but I must not go farther. I dare not step upon your country. I will call the Turtle. He will take you to your own people. Then the Terrible Person sang a song — The Song of the Waters — and the Turtle came to the top of the Big-water near them.

"Looks-at-the-stars did not know that there were such Turtle people as this one that came when the Terrible Person sang. This one was as large as a buffalo robe, and painted with many colors.

"'What is it you want?' asked the Turtle.

"'I want you to take this Young-man to the land — to his own country. Let him sit upon your back, and you must swim high so the waves will not wash him from your shell.'

"'I will do the best I can,' said the Turtle, 'but the Young-man must sit still or he will make me tip.'

"The Terrible Person put Looks-at-the-stars upon the Turtle's back, and said: 'Good-by,

Young-man. Never tell where I live. If you do I will make Trouble come to you and stay a long time.'

"'Good-by,' said Looks-at-the-stars, 'you have treated me well.'

"The Turtle swam away and so fast was he that before the day was gone his feet touched the shore of the land. 'Get off my back now,' said the Turtle, 'and remember what the Terrible Person has told you. Good-by, Young-man. I must get back to my family.' Then he was gone in the Big-water.

"The people thought that Looks-at-the-stars was dead. His father and mother had mourned for him. His father had cut off his hair in his grief, and his mother would speak to none. Ho! they were glad to see Looks-at-the-stars alive. There was a feast and much dancing. They asked him many questions, and he answered them all — all, but one. He would never tell where the Terrible Person lived, and we do not know to this day. Looks-at-the-stars is dead.

Uncounted snows have passed since he died, but yet we do not know where he met the Terrible Person because he kept his promise. Ho!"

CA–MEE–NO–WA–SIT

CA–MEE–NO–WA–SIT

"WAS Win-to-coo, the Man-eater, the worst Person on the World when it was new, grandfather?" asked Eyes-in-the-water one night in the lodge.

"No," replied War Eagle. "There was another Person with evil ways. He was strong and his heart was as bad as Win-to-coo's, but I never saw him. He had left the World before I came. His name was Ca-mee-no-wa-sit, the Hairy Man. My grandfather told me that he had never seen Ca-mee-no-wa-sit, and grandfather lived many snows ago. So the Hairy Man must have been on the World when all the people were young. Those who saw him have never talked with me, but many of our old men have heard of him, and, of course, he did live long ago. He may still be alive in some other country, but I am sure it must be far off or some of our people would see him, for they travel a great deal.

"Wah-ki-oose was a great hunter. He was of our own people, and my grandfather has told me of him. One night he dreamed. A Fox talked to him as he slept. This is what the Fox said: 'There is an Owl on your lodge-poles, oh, Wah-ki-oose. He is calling you.' Then the Fox went away into the forest. Wah-ki-oose saw him dig a hole in the ground near the roots of a pine-tree. In the digging the Fox found a feather. He brought the feather to the lodge and laid it upon the breast of Wah-ki-oose. Then he said again: 'There's an Owl on your lodge-poles, Wah-ki-oose. He is calling you. I have spoken.' As soon as he finished speaking the Fox went away in the night, and Wah-ki-oose saw him no more.

"The night was old when Wah-ki-oose awakened. 'Whoooo-Whoooo-Who-Whoo,' said an Owl right over his head. Yes, there was an Owl on the lodge-poles, and he was calling, as the Fox had said.

"Ho! Wah-ki-oose was frightened. That is always bad, to have an Owl call from the lodge-poles. Wah-ki-oose sat up and a feather fell to his knees. It was the feather that the Fox had laid upon his breast, and it was from the wing of the Thunder Bird — Ho!

"As soon as Wah-ki-oose sat up the Owl flew away from the lodge and did not call again, but fear was upon Wah-ki-oose. His heart was on the ground, and he was afraid. Finally the Sun came and looked in through the lodge door. It was in the summer, and as the Sun warmed the World, a Butterfly flew within and settled upon the youngest son of Wah-ki-oose. Ho! that was bad — very bad, and Wah-ki-oose watched the Butterfly fan the sleeping child with his wings. Slowly the wings moved in the bright sunlight and Wah-ki-oose knew that the child would die. He was sad. He thought he would take the little boy and go

101

away from there — far away. He lifted the sleeping child from the ground to his shoulders and ran through the forest. He saw the Fox, but he did not speak to him. He saw the Owl, too, but he did not go near him. All of the day he travelled toward the West until, when the day was old, he came to the plains.

"Far out in the open country he saw something moving and watched it. It looked like a man, and Wah-ki-oose was hungry. 'Perhaps that man's lodge is near. I will go to him and ask him to give us something to eat. Yes, I will speak to him,' he said to himself. 'Even if he is an enemy he will not refuse food.'

"When he was yet far from the Person he stopped, for the Person had held up his hand in warning. Then Wah-ki-oose saw that it was Ca-mee-no-wa-sit, the Hairy Man, and fear was in his heart. He could not move. He stood and gazed at the awful Person, and then Ca-mee-no-wa-sit waved his hand as though it held a knife. Suddenly Wah-ki-oose felt his shoulder growing warm and looked to see why it was so. It was blood. Yes, it was blood on his shoulder that made it warm, and the little boy was dead. Ca-mee-no-wa-sit had killed him. Ho! Wah-ki-oose turned to run, but the Hairy Man made another motion with his empty hand, and the runner fell bleeding upon the ground. He died there, and our people found them both — Wah-ki-oose and the boy— dead upon the plain.

"The Fox knew, and the Owl had told the truth. Even the Butterfly had given his warning, but Wah-ki-oose thought he could escape by running. What is to be, will be. Ho!"

STRIKES–AND–KILLS

STRIKES–AND–KILLS

"HAVE I ever told you the story of Strikes-and-kills?" asked War Eagle.

"No, grandfather," said Buffalo-calf. "Tell us the story."

"My grandfather knew a woman who was related to Strikes-and-kills," began War Eagle. "The woman was old when my grandfather was born, but she told him the story that I will tell you.

"The father of Strikes-and-kills lost his life in our wars with the Sioux. Strikes-and-kills had seen but four snows when his father fell in battle, and there was no one to kill meat for the family. People gave them meat, of course, but that is never the same as killing it yourself. Sometimes the meat that is given is not of the best, and Strikes-and-kills was proud. When he had seen eight snows his mother died and left him to take care of his brother, Little Bear, who had been on earth but a little more than four snows. Soon after his mother died the village moved, but Strikes-and-kills left his lodge standing. He said he would not go with the village. The old men that had known his father talked to him, but he said 'No, I am old enough now. I can kill my own meat and take care of my brother. I am going to stay here for a while.'

"So the village moved away. Where all the lodges had been there was nothing save the marks of the fires. Each morning Strikes-and-kills left his brother in the lodge and went hunting. Each day he killed two rabbits and caught a few fish in the river. But each night when he returned to the lodge with the meat and fish he found his little brother crying. One night he brought some willows to the lodge, and in the firelight made them into small hoops. These hoops he gave to Little Bear, and taught him how to roll them. The little boy played with the hoops and seemed happy, but every day he cried in the lodge, because he was lonesome. Strikes-and-kills was sorry for Little Bear, and one morning as he set out to hunt said: 'Come, my brother, I will take you with me. We will hunt together. I will walk slowly.'

So they started to hunt in the forest. Little Bear had his willow hoops strung on his arm, for he would not leave them behind, and kept talking and laughing. 'You must not talk, Little Bear,' said Strikes-and-kills. 'How can I kill rabbits when you talk and laugh. They hear your voice and run away and hide.'

"At last, they came to the shores of a large lake — a strange lake, as you shall see. They had travelled far, and Little Bear was tired. He began to cry, and Strikes-and-kills rolled the hoops for him. The shore of the lake was sandy and smooth, and the hoops rolled merrily. Sometimes a hoop would roll into the water and Little Bear would shout with delight when his brother stepped into the water and grabbed it before it floated away. 'I'll roll just one more hoop into the water, Little Bear,' said Strikes-and-kills. 'Then we must be going.'

The hoop danced over the sand, struck a rock, bounded high, staggered, reached the sand again, and then jumped into the water with a splash. Ho! a man in a canoe was there. They had not seen him before. No, not until the hoop struck the water and splashed it. The man scooped the hoop into his canoe with his paddle, and looked at them without speaking.

"'Do not take that hoop,' cried Strikes-and-kills. 'My brother will cry if you do.'

"'Come and get it, then,' said the man in the canoe, and he put his paddle-blade upon the shore to hold the canoe near the land.

"Strikes-and-kills stepped into the canoe to get the hoop and the man began to paddle away. 'Wait! I want to get out,' cried Strikes-and-kills. But the man paid no attention to his words and kept at paddling the canoe. The shore was far away now, and Ho! — where Little

Bear had been only a Wolf was standing. Then Strikes-and-kills knew that his brother had been changed into a Wolf. He looked to see what kind of a Person paddled the canoe. Ho! it was a Mountain Lion — not a Man-person, at all, but a Mountain Lion that paddled the canoe.

"At last the canoe touched the shore and the Lion-person told Strikes-and-kills to get out, and he did. 'Come with me,' said the Lion-person, picking up his canoe. He led the way to a dark cave in the rocks near the lake and entered. A young woman-lion was in the lodge and the Lion-person said: 'Daughter, I have brought you a Man-person. Keep him until he grows up, and then you may have him.' Then he covered Strikes-and-kills with his canoe and went to sleep in the lodge.

"The young Lion-woman was kind to Strikes-'and-kills. She let him out from under the canoe whenever her father was gone, but told him he must never try to run away. 'If you

111

do, my father will trail you and kill you,' she said.

Sometimes the Lion-person took his canoe to the lake, and then Strikes-and-kills walked about until he returned.

"At last he was a man. Strikes-and-kills had grown up, and he loved the Lion-woman. She had always been kind to him and so he loved her. He was a good hunter, and when her father, the Lion-person, forgot to bring meat to the lodge, Strikes-and-kills would kill a deer and bring in the meat. That made her love him, so one day they were married. Her father treated her badly, and sometimes Strikes-and-kills was made angry, but he dared not fight the Lion-person even when he abused her in the lodge.

"One day Strikes-and-kills was looking for service-berry bushes. He wanted to make some arrows, and complained because all the bushes grew crooked limbs. 'I know where there are plenty of straight ones,' said the Lion-person.

'Get into my canoe and I 'll take you to them.'
So Strikes-and-kills got into the canoe and the
Lion-person paddled away. They had been long
upon the lake when at last they reached an
island. 'Get out,' said the Lion-person. 'You
will find plenty of straight service-berry bushes
on this island.'

Strikes-and-kills got out of the canoe, but as
soon as he was on the land the Lion-person
paddled away. 'Wait,' called Strikes-and-kills.
'Wait for me.'

"'I 'll leave you for the Eagles. They will
pick your bones,' answered the Lion-person,
and kept paddling the canoe. Strikes-and-kills
thought of his wife, the Lion-woman. He called
and begged the Lion-person to come back, but
he would not come, nor answer.

"Gulls flew about the island and at last an
Eagle came and sat upon a limb of a dead tree
near the water. There was a large rock under
the tree, and on the rock sat a White Gull.

"'Kill that Eagle,' said the White Gull to

113

Strikes-and-kills. 'Kill him before he flies away.'

"Strikes-and-kills fitted an arrow to his bow-string. ZIPPP! went the arrow, and the Eagle fell dead.

"'Now take his skin from his body before it grows cold,' said the White Gull.

"'Who are you?' asked Strikes-and-kills as he began to take the skin from the Eagle's body.

"'I am *Old*-man,' said the White Gull. 'I saw it all. I know all about it. That's a mean Person, that Lion-man, but you shall go back to your lodge — back to your wife and stay there.'

"When Strikes-and-kills had taken the skin from the Eagle's body, he looked at the White Gull to see what he wanted him to do next.

"'Now crawl into the Eagle's skin,' said the White Gull. 'It will stretch and fit you as well as it did the Eagle.'

"Strikes-and-kills crawled into the skin, as

114

the White Gull told him he must, and the skin did stretch and did fit him as well as it had fitted the Eagle.

"'Now,' said the White Gull, 'fly to your lodge and see if you can get along with your father-in-law. Good-by.'

"Strikes-and-kills took a big stone in his talons and flew high up in the air. He went up, up, up until he was very high above the water, and then he headed for his lodge with the big stone in his talons. Away out on the waters of the lake there was a speck. Strikes-and-kills knew it was the canoe of the Lion-person, so he flew straight over it, and when he was high above the canoe and right over the head of the Lion-person, he let go of the big rock. SWOW! HO! the big rock missed the head of the Lion-person, but went straight through the bottom of the bark canoe. HO! the Lion-person was in the water. The broken canoe would not carry him. There was a great splashing! HO! Strikes-and-kills flew away and left the Lion-person to swim to the land or die there in the water.

"When Strikes-and-kills reached the lodge he told his wife what had happened, and how he had treated her father. 'You did well,' she said. 'But the water will not kill my father. Listen. I will tell you a great secret. Go to the shore of the lake and you will see a dead pine-tree. There is a great rock near that tree, and in the tree-top is an Eagle's nest. Listen well to my words, now. My father keeps his heart in that nest in the top of the dead pine-tree. If you can kill his heart, he will die, but as long as his heart lives, so will he live. You must be brave and careful for there are two Wicked Snakes that guard the tree-of-the-nest. After you pass them you will meet two bad-hearted Mountain Lions that always watch the tree-of-the-nest with the Snakes. These two Lions are my father's brothers. They know his heart is in the Eagle's nest, and will fight you if they find you near the tree. Now, be careful. Do not lose your life. Be brave and try to kill my father's heart, but keep your life. It is time my father came to the lodge, now. You had better go away and save trouble. I will be here waiting for you whenever you come for me.'

"Strikes-and-kills went into the forest. He was thinking as he walked. How could he kill the heart of the Lion-person? He thought of many ways, but, at last, he knew what he would do. He hunted for a fat deer and killed him. Then he cut the deer into pieces and made four packs of the meat. Two of the packs were large and two were small. He tied the four packs of meat with bark, and with them upon his back, went toward the lake. He was careful. He did not want to lose his life, so he was long in finding the tree-of-the-nest. But at last he saw it far ahead and commenced to walk toward it. First he must find the Wicked Snakes — he knew that — but before he saw anything that warned him, a Big Snake raised his head

117

from behind a log near him. 'What do you want here, young man?' said the Snake.

"'I have come to feed you some meat,' said Strikes-and-kills. 'I know what your business is, and that you do not have much time to hunt.' He tossed one of the small packs of meat to the Snake, and passed on. Soon he met the other Snake.

"'Stop where you are! You can go no farther. Who are you?'

"'I am the son-in-law of the man whose heart is in the nest,' said Strikes-and-kills. 'I have brought you meat to eat.' The Snake believed him and Strikes-and-kills went on. He was near the tree. His heart was beating fast. HO! two big Mountain Lions stood before him, their long tails swaying from side to side, and their green eyes glaring in the forest's light. HO! Together they came to meet him. 'Who are you?' asked the largest one of the Lions.

"'I am Strikes-and-kills, the son-in-law of the one whose heart is in the nest. I am a relation of yours, for his daughter is my wife. See! I have brought you meat,' and he dropped the two remaining packs of meat before him.

"'We are hungry,' said the Smaller Lion. 'We are glad that you thought of us. Where is our brother that he forgets us?'

"'He has gone on a long journey in his canoe,' said Strikes-and-kills. 'I have come in his place, for I feared you might be hungry.'

"The hungry Lions began to eat the meat and then Strikes-and-kills went on. In a short time he reached the tree, and, taking his bone-knife in his mouth, began to climb. If he could but reach the nest before the Lions finished eating the meat, all would be well, for, if he killed the heart in the nest, he could kill the two lions easily. He knew that and hurried. At last he reached the nest and looked in. There, beating in the light of day, was the heart of his

father-in-law, the Lion-person. SWOW! he
drove his knife into the heart once, twice, three
times, four times! Then it stopped beating.
The heart was dead.

"Strikes-and-kills climbed down to the
ground. He saw neither the Lions nor the
Wicked Snakes, but went to the lodge without
meeting any Person. His wife ran to meet
him. 'He's dead,' she cried. 'My father is
dead! He dropped down dead in the lodge.'

"'Yes,' said Strikes-and-kills. 'I killed his
heart. It was then that he died. Now come
with me, for I must look for my brother. I
know where I left him. We must see if he is
still there.'

"They travelled together for many days and
nights. At last, they came to the spot where
Strikes-and-kills had left Little Bear. 'Perhaps he is a Wolf, now,' said Strikes-and-kills,
'but I shall know him.'

Not a Person was in sight. They looked

about carefully. Finally they saw a King-fisher sitting on the limb of a tree near the water.

"'Have you seen my brother about here?' asked Strikes-and-kills of the Kingfisher.

"'No,' said the Kingfisher. 'I have seen no persons around here, and I have been here a long time. I live here.'

"'What are you doing here?' asked Strikes-and-kills.

"'Why, I'm making my living and minding my own business. Just now I am trying to catch one of those small fishes. If you won't come any closer maybe they'd come nearer the top.'

"'Have you *heard* anything of my brother around here?' asked Strikes-and-kills.

"'Well,' said the Kingfisher, 'there are some queer noises down there in the water. Lots of strange talking goes on down there in the lake. I often hear it.'

121

"'When do you hear it? What part of the day?' asked Strikes-and-kills.

"'Oh, mostly before the Sun comes with the Day. But it won't do you any good to listen. They are not your kind that speak.'

"HO!"

OLD–MAN'S COURTING

OLD–MAN'S COURTING

"TO–NIGHT the North-wind is blowing," said War Eagle. "Grandmother, put some big sticks upon the fire, for I will tell our grandchildren of *Old*-man's courting."

Grandmother made the fire burn brightly. It snapped and popped as though inviting a tale of mystery, and War Eagle smiled as he laid his pipe away and straightened his back-rest.

"It was a stormy day," he began. "Out on the plains the snow was piling in drifts. Deep in the forests the snow came down from the sky, and even there the breath of the North did not let it lie still; even there the snow-drifts piled among the trees. The Snow-shoe-rabbit, white and scared, hid in the bushes and in hollow logs upon the ground. The Wolf could not travel. The Deer-people and the Elk-people tramped great patches in the snow and waited there for a Chinook wind to come.

"At last it was ended. The North-wind was still. Hardly a sound was in the air. Even the Echo-people slept so soundly that nothing wakened them. The Owl hooted when the night came, but his voice was alone. None of the Echo-people answered — the snow was too deep. They were sleeping and did not hear. Then the sky cleared and the Moon came out to look upon the World. As soon as the Moon-light came the Shadow-people crept from their lodges and stood upon the snow, mocking things beside them as the Echo-people mock the voices of men in the mountains and along the rivers. I think the Shadow-people and the Echo-people are relations, for they have ways that are much the same — they are mimics in all they do.

"All through the awful storm a man was travelling. It was *Old*-man, and he wallowed through the deep snow as the Bear would, if the Bear were out, but he wasn't. He had more sense. The snow was too deep. The Bear was sleeping, as he always does when the snows are deep. It was *Old*-man that taught the Bear to do that way, but he was not wise enough to do it himself. It is strange that those who are able to tell others what to do, do not always follow their own teaching.

So *Old*-man was travelling during the storm. He was tired and hungry when he reached the forest. He had been out on the plains and had found nothing to eat, and the night was coming when he entered the forest. None of the Forest-people were stirring, and at last the night came on. The Moon climbed into the sky to watch the World until the Sun came with the Day. Finally *Old*-man found a big spruce-tree whose branches reached nearly to the ground. They did reach the snow that was piled about them. He pushed the branches aside and looked in. The ground was bare and dry about the tree. No snow had entered there. 'Ho!' he cried,

127

'I'll camp here. I'll spend the night right here, I guess.'

"A Snow-shoe-rabbit ran out as *Old*-man entered, and he cried: 'Wait. Wait, my brother. I am lonesome. I want to talk to you.'

"'I'm afraid of you,' said the Rabbit, as he ran away through the snow.

"'I made you,' said *Old*-man.

"'I know you did, but you made more enemies for me than for anybody else; so I have to be careful. I'll find another place to sleep.' And he ran away.

"'Everybody is afraid of me, and if it were not for me there wouldn't be anybody,' said *Old*-man, as he leaned back against the tree. Through the overhanging branches he could see the Shadow-people standing on the snow, everywhere. They scarcely moved, but waited patiently for the Breeze to stir the trees or move the branches overhead; then they danced as long as the Breeze sang. An Owl hooted away in the snowy forest. 'Whoooo —Whoooo — Who-Who!'

"'Hey, you Owl-person! Come here. I want to talk to Somebody,' cried *Old*-man. But the Owl didn't come. He didn't even answer; if he heard the call. But he kept at his hooting in the night.

"It was warm under the spruce-tree and *Old*-man's eyelids drooped, shut tight, opened, drooped once more — and he was asleep. Ho! he was snoring loudly.

"Something stirred on the other side of the spruce-tree. It was not loud, but there was a noise behind *Old*-man, on the other side of the tree. 'Who is that?' asked *Old*-man.

"'Myself and my daughter,' said a voice behind the tree.

"'Who are you?'

"The voice didn't answer.

"'Do you live here?' asked *Old*-man.

"'Yes,' said the voice.

"'She's pretty — very pretty,' said *Old*-man.

129

"'Who's pretty?' asked the voice.

"'Why, your daughter, of course,' said *Old*-man. 'I'm a great hunter, too. I know many things.'

"The voice said nothing.

"'I say I am a great hunter and I have no woman,' said *Old*-man. But the voice did not reply.

"'Say! Can't you hear me? I say I have no woman and I am looking for one. I am a great hunter and will be good to any woman I get.'

"All was still. No Person answered.

"'Give me your daughter,' begged *Old*-man. 'I'll be good to her and take care of her.'

"'You'll have to talk to my daughter,' said the voice.

"'Will you not talk to me, woman?' asked *Old*-man. 'Please talk to me, for I am in love with you, and I want you.'

"'Yes, and I will go with you, if you will be kind to me,' said the young woman.

"'Well, I 'll be good to you, of course. Come and sit beside me.'

"She came and sat beside him. He tried to put his arm about her. 'Don't do that,' she cried. 'You mustn't do that.'

"'Why not?'

"'Because I am hardly a Person, yet.'

"'Can't I tell a Person when I see her? Can't I tell a pretty woman with my eyes?'

"'Oh, you think you can,' said the young woman, 'but I am not quite a Person. You cannot court me any more until twelve days have passed — then I 'll be a Person.'

"'Do you think I 'm going to sit here and wait for twelve days? How can I wait twelve days?'

"No voice answered him.

"'Well, how can I?' he repeated.

"No answer.

"He grabbed at the woman. WHIRRRRR! a blue grouse flew from beneath the spruce-tree with a great noise. *Old*-man had *grabbed* in his sleep and had fallen over on his face. When he sat up again he felt something soft in his hand. It was full of the tail-feathers of the bird that was gone. Ho!"

BILLY BENT AND THE ECHO PEOPLE

Y OU don't know Billy Bent; but I know
him. Billy lives in the Rocky Mountains
where the Missouri River is born and where
the game trails wander along the creeks that
feed the tributaries of that wonderful river.
Billy loves to follow these trails, for they pass
through strange places—places that are as
silent and as wild as they were when Christopher
Columbus sailed from Spain.

Billy told me once, "If you sit down when
you come to one of those lonesome places and
sit very still a long time and listen, you'll hear
things."

"What kind of things, Billy?" I asked.

"Oh, little things," he answered.

Then I began to watch Billy. I tried to hear
the "little things" in lonesome places, too.

For a long time I couldn't hear anything,

135

but now I can. And I know where Billy learned to look and listen, besides. I'll tell you about it.

One day when Billy was ten years old he was sitting on a log that had fallen across a deer trail. The log had been there so long that it was worn where the trail crossed it. He straddled it so that by turning his head he could look both ways along the trail.

There was a little meadow-place not far from the log, and an old doe lived there with two spotted fawns. Billy was watching for her. He knew that the fawns were hidden somewhere in the long grass in the little meadow, because he had seen them several times before. The afternoon was warm, and mosquitoes bothered him a good deal, but he knew that the fawns would not move from their beds until their mother came to them; so he waited.

A rabbit bobbed across the trail not far from Billy. When it entered the bushes on the other side, it turned suddenly, and almost ran against

136

Billy's foot. Something had scared the rabbit. Billy's eyes searched the bushes to see what it could be that had frightened the rabbit, and he was about to give it up when he thought he saw a man's nose.

Sometimes shadows and leaves and bark and sunshine play tricks in the forest, and Billy knew that; but he looked steadily at the nose and waited. Then he thought he saw an eye, but it did not wink. It did not move but stared straight ahead.

"If it's a man's eye it's got to wink sometime." That is what Billy told me he thought as he watched.

"There were more mosquitoes than ever," said Billy. "But I didn't dare to brush them off for fear that eye would wink and I wouldn't see it."

At last a breeze moved the bushes ever so little, but enough to show Billy a braid of hair. And besides, the eye winked, or he thought it did.

"Hello," whispered Billy.

"How, Looks-and-listens." The words were so soft spoken that they barely reached Billy.

It was Good Voice, an aged Indian that Billy knew. And there is where it began—I mean, there is where Billy began really to look and listen.

The Indians called him "Looks-and-listens," because they had often seen him alone in the mountains, but he has told me that he learned how to hear and see things from Good Voice, and that it began that day.

"What are you doing here?" asked Good Voice.

"Oh, just waiting and listening for things," Billy told him.

"There are many sounds to hear, and strange things to see for those who have good ears and eyes," said the Indian. "What do you like best of all that you hear?"

"I don't know their names," said Billy.

And just then a raven flew over their heads

138

and said, "Caw, caw!" almost the same as the call of a crow, only deeper in tone. "Caw, caw!" said the raven. And, "Caw, caw!" came an answer, a little fainter, hollower, and farther away.

Billy smiled and looked at Good Voice. "That's one of the things I like to hear—that other voice that answers the raven. It is not a bird nor a man nor anything, but it's one of those strange things that speak where quiet lives. Do you know what it is that answers ravens and others that make noises in still places, Good Voice?"

"Yes," said the Indian. "I know who speaks as you say. They are the Echo People."

"Where do they live?" asked Billy.

"In the silent places," said the Indian.

"Have you ever seen them, Good Voice?"

"No, I have never seen them, but I have often talked to them. They are wonderful mimics, the Echo People, and they love to laugh but they will not, unless you laugh and make them happy with your own mood. They never break the stillness themselves, but hide behind the great rocks near the rivers to mock those who pass and use their voices. They speak every language, make every note the large birds make, and answer the wolves and coyotes with their own words. They sleep until disturbed, and their tribes do not move but stay in one place forever.

"Come, I will show you a camp where the Echo People have wonderful voices. Those same voices were there when my grandfather was a boy. They are still there and are sleeping, but I will wake them that you may hear them speak. Come."

It was after sundown when Good Voice whispered, "We are nearly there. Make no noise until I speak to the Echo People. When they are startled many speak in this camp."

Billy walked softly. The trail suddenly turned and went down a steep hill until it

140

reached the bank of a river. Then it began to follow the stream as though it did not like to leave it again.

Good Voice stopped and held up his hand. Billy stood still. There were two great cliffs of rock not far away. One was across the river, and the other reached much higher upon the mountain on the side where Good Voice and Billy were. Both of the cliffs were colored red and yellow and white, and even green, by the minerals in the rock, and they looked very beautiful in the soft light after the sun had gone.

"Whooooo! Hey! Hey!" Good Voice yelled. "Ho! Ho! Ho! Echo People. Looks-and-listens has come to your camp!"

"Wooooo! Hey! Hey! Ho! Ho! Ho! Echo People. Looks-and-listens has come to your camp—camp—camp," replied the Echoes, using his exact words and repeating the last over and over again, until the voices could scarcely be heard.

141

"Have they run away?" asked Billy.

"No," said Good Voice. "Those that spoke last are farther away than the ones who first answered me. This is a large camp of the Echo People. It covers much ground. Those who live on the outskirts of the camp did not answer me—they answered the others who were near us. They are always at home. They never go away, but they are great sleepers and you would think they would not wake so quickly. They all awake at once and all answer disturbers of the silence. It is their way. I have never seen them, nor did my grandfather who lived before me."

"I am glad I know where they live, Good Voice," said Billy. "I shall come here often and speak that they may awake and answer me. I must go home now. Can I come to your lodge some day?"

"Yes," said Good Voice. "Come."

Billy turned back over the dark trail toward

his home. The shadows were deep in the forest and along the river, but he was not afraid. "I'll ask old Good Voice about the Shadows when I visit him," he said aloud, as he climbed a steep hill. For Billy sometimes talks to himself.

OLD-MAN AND THE SUN-DANCE

OLD-MAN AND THE SUN-DANCE

THERE were great preparations for a sun-dance in the village. The leaves upon the trees were nearly full grown, and it was time for the dance. The poles for the sacred lodge had been cut and were ready for use. Everyone was talking of the coming event, and when the children came to War Eagle's lodge they were full of excitement and anxious to learn of the sun-dance.

"The sun-dance is old," said War Eagle. "Many people have sun-dances. No man can tell who first made the sun-dance." He put away his pipe and was silent for a moment. Then he said:

"Once, long ago, *Old*-man was travelling in the forest. The day was warm and he was thirsty. He stopped at a creek to drink, and after drinking sat still and listened to the water rippling over the stones on the creek's bottom. He was tired. 'High Ho!' he yawned, and went to sleep there by the water. When he wakened he heard singing. It was soft and low. There were no loud voices among the singers. He listened, but could see no people. 'Say, you!' he called, 'who is doing that singing?' But there was no answer. He called again, but no answer came, and the singing continued. 'That is queer,' he said. 'There's singing going on and I can see no singers.' He stood up and looked about. Not a man was in sight. He walked down the creek a little way and there stood still to listen again. No sound came to him. The singing had ceased. 'They must be up the creek,' he said aloud. 'I'll go up that way and find them.'

"He passed the place where he had slept without stopping and went on up the stream. Then he stopped and looked about. He stood very still to listen, but there was no sound in the forest save that which was made by a wood-

148

pecker on a tree-top. 'That is funny,' said *Old*-man. 'I 'm sure that I heard singing. I 'll go back to the place where I slept and listen once more.'

"He went back and stopped to listen. The same sound of singing came to him. 'It 's right here,' he muttered, 'but I can see no people.' He began to look among the willows that grew along the creek and in the long grass. At last he saw the head and horns of a Bull-elk. The Elk had died in winter and the wolves had cleaned the bones of all meat and hide, but the head was still covered with the skin. The eyes were gone and the skull smelled badly. *Old*-man stood still and looked at the head of the Bull-elk for a long time. And then he saw a Fly go into the head through one of the eye-holes in the skull. 'Ah!' he cried, 'it is in there. The singing is in there.'

"He knelt beside the Elk's head and listened. Yes, there was singing inside. Many low voices were singing the same song. Just then a Fly

149

came out and *Old*-man asked: 'What is going on in there?'

"'Oh, it's a sun-dance,' answered the Fly and went away.

"*Old*-man waited until another Fly came out and then he said: 'I want to go in to that sun-dance. Tell me how to get in.'

"'You are too large,' said the Fly.

"'No, I am not too large,' declared *Old*-man— 'not if you will show me the way—not if you will help me.'

"'Well, STOOP LOW, AND KEEP YOUR EYES SHUT TIGHT,' said the Fly. 'Perhaps you can get in, but be sure to keep your eyes shut until I tell you to open them.'

"'All right. I'm ready,' laughed *Old*-man.

"'No, you are *not* ready,' answered the Fly. 'You are laughing.'

"'I'll stop laughing. I *have* stopped,' declared *Old*-man, and he stooped low and closed his eyes. He began to squeeze himself into the eye-hole after the Fly. The singing was very near, but

Old-man was not yet inside. The Fly had not told him to open his eyes, but he did. Oh-Ho! —he *did*—and he was stuck hard and fast there. He could not move. He could not get his head out of the eye-hole in the Bull-elk's head. Oh-ho! *Old*-man was in trouble. He began to cry and twist and turn, but he could not get out. He was stuck tight. At last he stood up with the Bull-elk's head stuck fast to his own. He began to run through the forest like one who has lost his reason. SWOW! he ran into a tree.

"'What tree are you?' he asked.

"'I'm a pine,' said the tree.

"*Old*-man ran on until SWOW! he bumped into another tree.

"'What tree are *you?*' he cried.

"'I'm a spruce,' replied the tree.

"Away he went again, running fast and faster through the forest when SWOW! he struck another tree.

"'What tree are you?' he asked.

"'I 'm a birch,' said the tree. 'I grow near the water.'

"'Good!' said *Old*-man, 'but where is the water?'

"'Right ahead of you,' replied the birch-tree. 'Right straight ahead, if you are able to get it.'

"*Old*-man waded out into the water. It was a lake of water and the birch-tree grew near it. The water grew deeper and deeper as *Old*-man waded, but he could not drink because of the Bull-elk's head that was fast upon his own. He walked farther out in the water. 'How deep am I now, Oh Birch-tree?' he called.

"'You are up to your waist in the water,' answered the tree.

"'I can't drink yet,' whined *Old*-man, and waded still farther out in the water. 'Now, how deep am I?' he called.

"'The water is over your shoulders, and if you go farther you will die,' answered the tree.

"*Old*-man bent his head to try to drink.

"Then there was a great noise and an arrow struck the water near to *Old*-man's head and he ran—ran away into the forest with many of our people after him. They thought that he was a bull-elk swimming in the lake and chased him. He ran even faster than before. He was lucky for a long time, but finally SWOW! he ran into a fir tree and fell. The blow broke the Bull-elk's skull and it fell away from *Old*-man's head, but he did not know it. He was without his thoughts. His mind was asleep. The fir tree had hurt him. At last he sat up and looked about. Many people stood around him and they were laughing.

"The sun-dance is old. Ho!"

WHY THE DOGS HOWL AT NIGHT

WHY THE DOGS HOWL AT NIGHT

"HERE is some tobacco, grandfather," said Buffalo-calf. "We traded a robe for it at the fort. It is for you. We like to see you smoke your pipe."

"Yes, grandfather," agreed Eyes-in-the-water, "and we like it when you tell us stories of *Old*-man."

"Ah," said War Eagle, "I fear that I can tell you no more stories of *Old*-man. I will think while I smoke."

He lighted his pipe and smoked in silence while the children waited hopefully. At last, having finished with the pipe, he laid it away.

'*Old*-man made the Dog-people, of course," he said, straightening his back-rest. "You know that he made everything, but the Dogs have learned many things since they were made

157

—things that *Old*-man did not teach them—
things that he did not think of, perhaps.

"You have heard the Dogs howl at night.
You have wondered why they do that. They
are howling at the Dog-star which shines at
night with the other stars. The Dogs believe
that they have relations living on the Dog-
star, and speak to them with loud voices, for
the star is far away. The Dog-star comes close
to the world sometimes with the other stars.
It is then that the Dogs howl at night, for they
believe that they should speak to their people
on the star whenever they are near enough to
hear their voices.

"When people believe that such things are
right, and do them for that reason, we should
not complain. That is why we never object
when our Dogs howl at night. We know why
they do it, and we know that they believe that
it is the right thing to do. We know that they
were told to do it. I will tell you the story:

"Once, a long time ago, the Dogs had a great

chief. He was wise. He was just. He was strong and he thought of ways to make his people better. The Dog-people loved their chief, and he lived to be very old. His hair grew white with the snows that passed his head, and that is the mark of Manitou's esteem. The chief-dog made long journeys into the mountains, alone. He went there to dream and to think. Voices spoke to him on the high mountains, but it was always night when the voices spoke. At last he learned where the voices came from, but he did not speak of the voices to his people until he was growing old. One day he called a council, and when the Dogs were all assembled he said:

"'I am growing old. I can not live forever.' The Dogs began to whine at this, but he told them to stop it, and they did stop it. 'Listen,' said the chief, and they listened. 'I have spent much time alone,' he told them. 'Sometimes voices have spoken to me, but for a long time I did not know whose voice it was that spoke, nor

159

where it came from. I always listened, and always the voice came to me at night. One night I was alone in the mountains. It was winter. The snows were deep and crusted. They would bear my weight everywhere. The cold of the night was terrible. My breath was white and my hair was frosted from it. No wind was stirring and the stars seemed to be just above the tree-tops a little way. They were bluish-white and large, and very near. Not a sound was in the air except my own footsteps on the snow-crust. The strange, moving lights that sometimes burn in the north were dancing that night in a sheen of yellow-green. They ran along the mountain tops, and reached far up into the sky, but when I had climbed to where they seemed to have stopped, they were gone—gone to a higher mountain farther away toward the north. I followed, because I thought that the voices that I had heard so many times came from those strange, moving lights. I stopped, at last, on a mountain top and looked at the strange

lights until the cold would let me stand no
longer. I started to move away when a voice
said: "Why do you never speak to your relations here?"

""'"Where?" I asked.

""'"Here," replied the voice.

"'I looked carefully, but could see nothing,
nobody. I had often heard that same voice,
but never so plainly. "I cannot see you," I
said.

""'"I am here with many of your relations,"
replied the voice, and then I saw a star that
seemed to move in the sky. It seemed very close
and I watched there in the bitter cold—watched
and listened. I heard our relations on the star—
many of them. They were howling—trying to
make us hear them, but their voices were faint
and seemed far away. Then the voice spoke
again. "Hear my people?" it asked.

""'"I hear them, but faintly," I answered.
"Are you with them on the star?"

""'"Yes, I am their chief," said the voice.

161

"I would that your people and mine might be close friends for we are alike."

"'I was freezing. I told the Chief-dog that I could stay there no longer. I went away, but since that night I have heard the voice many times. Before I die I want to make friends with our relations on that star, and I ask that the strongest among the young Dogs stand before me.'

"There was much talking among the Dogs— much arguing between the old ones, but at last a large Dog came and stood before the chief. He was young and strong and sound.

"'Are you the strongest Dog among the young ones?' asked the chief.

"'They say that I am,' replied the Dog. 'My name is Friend and I would serve you.'

"'Good,' said the chief. 'I am going to send a present to the chief-dog on the star. The journey will be a long one. You will need all the snows that are before you, and you will be old ere you return to us. I will show you the

way, but I warn you that you must go alone.
Are you willing to make the journey?'

"'I am willing, chief,' Friend answered. 'I
am willing and ready to go.'

"'Good,' said the chief. 'Let all you people
go now and bring the finest piece of back-fat
that you can find. Go at once.'

"The Dogs went away and began to hunt for
pieces of back-fat. Whenever a Dog found a
fine piece he brought it to the chief. Soon a
great pile of back-fat was before him, and the
chief carefully examined every piece. At last
he found one that suited him. It was hard and
white, and from a fresh-killed buffalo cow.

"'This will do,' he said. 'Now get me a
strong string of rawhide.'

"They brought the string. 'Come close,
Friend,' said the chief, and the young dog stood
close. The chief tied the back-fat about the
neck of Friend with the rawhide string.

"Then he turned and spoke to the Dogs:

"'We are going away, Friend and I, but I

shall return soon. Friend will not come back for a long time; perhaps not until after I am dead. Whenever he comes you must honor him, and help him, for he will be old, maybe. Come, Friend,' and they went away.

"Many days passed and then the chief came back to his people. He did not speak of Friend or of his journey. Most of the Dogs had forgotten about it, when one day the chief called another council. When all the Dogs had arrived the chief said:

"'I have made a mistake and I would mend it. Friend has gone to the Dog-star with a present for the chief-dog. Friend is young now, but he may be old when he returns, for nobody has ever made so long a journey. We know him now, but age changes all things. He may have war on the way and the scars of battle help time to disfigure bodies. I should have marked that Dog so that we would know him, no matter when he returns to us. I have thought about this, and I ask that the swiftest Dog among you stand before me.'

"The Dogs began to talk and there was some quarrelling among them, but finally a Dog stood before the chief, who asked: 'Are you the swiftest Dog among my people?'

"'They say that I am—all but one— He thinks that he can beat me,' replied the dog. 'My name is South-wind.'

"'What is the name of the Dog who thinks that he can beat you running?' asked the chief.

"'North-wind,' replied the dog.

"Then the chief called for North-wind and he came and stood before his chief with South-wind.

"'I have use for the swiftest among my people,' said the chief. 'I must not make a mistake in my choice. Run to the top of that hill yonder, and the one that returns first to me, shall be my messenger.'

"Away went the two fast Dogs while the rest

watched the race, but South-wind was first to return to the chief.

"'Good,' he said. 'South-wind, I want you to take the trail of Friend and bring him back. I will show you the way that he went. Come.' And the chief and South-wind left the rest there at the council. The chief returned soon, but most of the Dogs had already gone to their lodges.

"It was nearly winter before South-wind returned with Friend, but the chief called a council at once. He asked the Dogs to bring with them the best piece of back-fat that they could find. They came, of course, and they all brought a piece of back-fat. They were wondering and there was much talking among them. At last, when they were all there, the chief spoke:

"'I will send Friend upon his journey once more, but when he returns every dog will know him, no matter how long he is gone from among us. Even our grandchildren will know him although they may not be born. We shall tell our children of Friend's long journey and they, in turn, will tell their children, until at last our messenger returns to his people. He selected the best piece of back-fat from the pile that the Dogs had brought to the council and tied it about the neck of Friend in place of the other piece which was becoming old. 'Now,' he said, 'I have made a musk for Friend. There is no other that is like it. There never can be. You cannot mistake it. When you have smelled it you will know it ever afterward. I have made the musk from roots and herbs of the forest. The secret of its making will die with me lest it become common. I want every Dog to come and smell this musk,' and they came and smelled it. 'I need not tell you to remember this smell,' said the chief. 'I know that you will never forget it.'

"Then he took a stick and dipped it into the musk that he had made. He rubbed the stick upon the root of Friend's tail and said: 'There.

That will never come off. We shall know you by that smell and we shall look for you as long as we live. After we are dead our children will look for you as we did. Now let us eat the rest of this pile of back-fat. Let us feast, and from the feast send our gift to our relations on the Dog-star.'

"They ate the back-fat and told stories until nearly morning. At last the chief said: 'Friend, is there anything that you want done while you are away?'

"'Yes,' replied Friend, 'there is. I wish that our people would howl once in a while at night, for the trail to the Dog-star is lonesome. I could hear the voices of our relations on the star before I returned, but my own people were silent. Let them answer our relations on the Dog-star. It will please them and cheer me.'

"'Good,' said the chief. 'It will be done. Do you hear, my people? Once in a while you must howl at night when the Dog-star is near. Remember that all your lives. Remember, also, to look for Friend and whenever you see a strange Dog, see if he wears the musk that I have put upon Friend. Do not fail in this. Always look for Friend until you die.'

"And they do. Ho."